'We had been told, c
that we were going t
conferred on us by s

We were able to verify that all this was true, and, because it was true, we did not hesitate to shed our quota of blood, to sacrifice our youth and our hopes. We regretted nothing, but whereas we over here are inspired by this frame of mind, I am told that in Rome factions and conspiracies are rife, that treachery flourishes and that many people in their uncertainty and confusion lend a ready ear to the dire temptations of relinquishment and vilify our action.

I cannot believe that all this is true and yet recent wars have shown how pernicious such a state of mind could be and to where it could lead.

Make haste to reassure me, I beg you and tell me that our fellow citizens understand us, support us and protect us as we ourselves are protecting the glory of the Empire.

If it should be otherwise, if we should have to leave our bleached bones on these desert sands in vain, then beware the anger of the Legion!'

Marcus Flavinius.
Centurion in the 2nd Cohort of the Augusta Legion to his cousin Tertellus in Rome, 1st Century AD.

Also by Leo Kessler in the *Wotan* series

SS PANZER BATTALION
DEATH'S HEAD
CLAWS OF STEEL

'In essence, we must take certain action if the Führer will not make peace before it is too late.'
'And that action?'
'*To overthrow Adolf Hitler*'

SS General Schellenberg to Major von Dodenburg
SS Battle Group WOTAN, December 1943

Leo Kessler

Guns at Cassino

Futura Publications Limited

A Futura Book

First published in Great Britain in 1975
by Futura Publications Limited

ISBN 0 8600 7101 4

Printed in Great Britain by
Cox & Wyman Ltd
London, Reading and Fakenham

Futura Publications Limited
49 Poland Street, London W1A 2LG

One: Cassino

'Gentlemen, this is where we are going to stand. I have no further orders from Smiling Albert than these – *stand and fight! Colonel Geier, C.O. Battle Group WOTAN to his officers, December 1943.*

ONE

The Leader turned to the sombre-eyed valet, waiting attentively at the door of his bedroom.

'You may go, Linge. I won't need you any further tonight.'

Linge, who was also a colonel in the SS, bowed. He knew the formula. His chief wanted to be alone with his mistress. The long boring evening at Obersalzberg was over. He would be glad to climb into his bed and sleep without interruption, leaving the Leader to enjoy the plump favours of the red-cheeked, ex-photographer's assistant.

'Good-night,' Linge said softly, omitting the usual, 'sleep well, my Leader.' Under the circumstances, it would seem an impertinence. As he closed the door of the bedroom behind him, he heard his chief call, '*Tschapperl*', that slightly contemptuous Bavarian pet name he had for his young mistress.

Eva was waiting for him in her absurd frilly bedroom which was a clear proof of the essential triviality of her mind – just as her conversation had been the whole evening in front of the big log fire. But then, the middle-aged Leader told himself, he could not afford to keep a clever woman as his mistress. As he often remarked to his cronies of the inner circle – Speer,

Hoffmann, and the like – an intelligent man should always take a primitive and stupid woman to satisfy his sexual needs.

He dismissed the thought from his mind. Tonight he must concentrate on his pleasure; after all that is why he had flown from his headquarters at the 'Wolf's Lair'. To enjoy a couple of days' leisure on the 'Mountain', forgetting the war, even the terrible mess on the Italian front. He let his gaze fall on her body, displayed as ordered, her ample breasts clearly visible through the silk nightdress, bought expressly for the purpose by Bormann in Paris. Eva's legs were already spread.

'Are you ready?' he asked, a slight catch in his guttural voice.

'Yes, Adolf,' Eva said on the bed and lowered her eyes. Even after all these years she could not get used to the strange forms of sexual pleasure enjoyed by the greatest man in Europe. She was naïve – another Gerdi Raubal. But Gerdi, his niece, was long dead: a suicide.

'Good,' he said, beginning to take off his tunic. 'Then take up your nightdress, please.'

She blushed and did as he commanded. She could hear him breathing a little harder now and out of the corner of her eyes, she could see how his fingers trembled as they fumbled with his tie. Finally he was naked and ready, his body pale and plump, so unlike the hard muscular firmness of that Italian officer so long ago.

'Open them – wider,' he ordered, his voice suddenly thick with lust, '*wider, I said.*'

Hastily she obeyed. For an instant she looked down at his black shock of hair, now lightly flecked with silver, as he slid his head the length of her white body. The Leader found what he sought. She gave a shudder of pleasure and disgust. Then she raised her gaze to the ceiling and let her body go limp so that he could have his way. Now the man, who commanded the destinies of two hundred and eighty million Europeans, crouched animal-like, with his head between her thighs. Adolf Hitler was taking his pleasure.

Eva Braun stiffled a yawn and reached for another chocolate. The Führer was still not tired. But the restless flickering of his dark eyes was gone. She had succeeded in satisfying him – thank God! Now she would have to entertain him until he felt it was time to retire to his own room. But the Führer was often like this, unable to sleep unless his personal physician Dr Morell, who kept injecting extracts from sheep testicles and Bulgarian peasant blood into the Führer, gave him yet more pills.

Now he sat there on one of her armchairs, clad in his pyjamas, his hair a little tousled still, brooding, it seemed. There was no sound save for that of the wind howling around the 'Mountain' and the steady stamp of the sentries from the 'Bodyguard' on the hard snow below.*

'What are you thinking about, Adolf?' she asked softly, savouring the name she never dare use save when they were alone in the privacy of her bedroom.

Hitler rose and stared out of the window at the Northern Lights, which were bathing the legendary Untersberg across the valley a dramatic crimson.

'The war,' he replied gruffly, 'what else but the war!'

'But you are on leave,' she protested gently and helped herself to another of the chocolates he had brought her. 'You must forget the war for a while.'

'I am never on leave. The Leader of the German people can never rest, day or night. When one controls the destinies of a great people there are two—'

'*Possibilities*,' she interrupted him cheekily, using his favourite opening gambit.

His harsh face broke into a slight grin.

'*Tschapperl!*' he said, his voice heavy with mock menace, 'what do you know of such things. But, perhaps you are right.' He returned to his chair again. 'Good, then Eva, you will amuse me – take my mind off the war. *Talk*.' He barked the word out like a military command.

Eva Braun was not offended. She was glad that she had been able to drag his mind away from the terrible conflict which had now been going on for over four years.

'Well,' she began, 'the last time *I* went on leave, I drove to Italy. That was just before the war.'

* The SS Regiment which bore the title of Bodyguard (*transl.*).

'Don't mention Italy to me. Those damned traitors!' he exclaimed.

She overheard the objection.

'But it was beautiful, Adolf,' she enthused. 'The sea, the buildings, the countryside! Now I can understand why Goethe said that every German desires to go south to Italy . . .'

Adolf Hitler sighed at such naïvety, but he let her talk his mind already wandering to the situation in Italy which had deteriorated rapidly ever since that traitor King Emmanuel had deposed his friend Mussolini and invited the Allies to invade his country. Things had been bad enough already, with the Bolsheviks steadily pushing his armies back towards Poland with no indication they could be stopped before they reached the frontiers of the Reich itself. But now the Allies were on his very doorstep too. If it had not been for the fact that their generals were too cautious, he might well have been battling with them now on the borders of the East Mark itself.* And the Wehrmacht simply did not have the men to spare to fight on two major fronts. What in devil's name was he going to do?

'We spent a day at Cassino,' Eva rambled on. Her mind was on that beautiful Italian Air Force officer who had ditched her Gestapo bodyguard and driven up to the great monastery on Route Six which snaked down the coast from Rome. 'It was beautiful. It was built by Saint Benedict – he's buried there. Then there is the high altar screen. It is supposed to have been done by Michelangelo—'

'That rank homosexual!' Hitler interrupted coarsely, tearing his mind from the miserable situation on the Italian front. 'If he had lived today, I would have had him placed in a concentration camp with the rest of those warm brothers!'

'But he was a really great artist,' she protested mildly. 'And Monte Cassino is a cultural treasure.'

Hitler held up his hand imperiously, suddenly very wide awake.

'What did you say?' he barked.

She looked at him, puzzled and alarmed at the sudden change in his mood.

'A cultural treasure, Adolf.'

* East Mark, Nazi terminology for Austria. (*transl.*).

Hitler sprang to his feet. He walked over to the massive picture window.

'A cultural treasure,' he echoed, staring out at the Northern Lights, shimmering now in all colours of the rainbow like the last act of the *Goetterdaemmerung*, staged by the young Wagner at Bayreuth. '*A cultural treasure*,' he repeated with more emphasis, the great idea slowly beginning to take shape in his fertile mind. 'Monte Cassino and the monastery dominating the major western coastal route to the Italian capital.'

Eva, sprawled out on the rumpled bed, chocolate in her plump hand, her mouth opened stupidly, stared at him in amazement, as Adolf Hitler strode to the door of her room, flung it open and yelled at the top of his tremendous voice:

'Linge . . . Linge! *Linge!* . . . Wake up General Jodl and my military staff . . . Tell them I want Kesselring on the phone *at once*.'

TWO

The stocky ex-artilleryman who was now in command in Italy rose to his feet hastily as Hitler entered the salon followed by Jodl and his adjutants.

The Führer seized the Field Marshal's right hand in both of his warmly.

'It is good of you to come immediately, Kesselring. I know how difficult it is to get away from the front, especially under present circumstances.'

'It is a great honour to be called here, my Führer,' Kesselring answered, a little embarrassed by the German Leader's hypnotic gaze.

Finally Hitler released his grip.

'But let us sit down.' He waved his hand round the salon.

'Thank you, my Führer.'

Kesselring sat down beneath the picturesque reclining nude which was said to be by Titian himself while Hitler lowered himself into one of the red upholstered chairs near the fireplace so that the light from the picture window fell over his shoulder and he would not need to wear the gold-rimmed spectacles he abhorred.

'Good, Kesselring, if you are ready?' Hitler threw a glance at his pale-faced clever Chief-of-Staff Colonel-General Jodl to ascertain if he were also ready. He was. 'Would you please fill us in quickly on the Italian situation?'

Kesselring, known by his staff behind his back as 'smiling Albert', was optimistic as always:

'The Tenth Army is well positioned, sir. We are blocking both the American Fifth Army and the Tommies' Eighth on both coastal routes leading to the capital and the north. I think we can safely say that General von Senger, the commander of the Tenth, has got the situation well in hand. Our positions are easily defensible – at least until the enemy can outnumber us three to one. Which is not the case at the moment. The only victory that they had been able to achieve is the capture of Peak 555 last week by the French.'

'Peak 555?' Hitler asked quickly. He prided himself on his intimate knowledge of all fronts; it annoyed him that he did not know immediately where the Peak was.

'It is to the south-east of Cassino, my Führer,' Kesselring explained. 'The French threw in a whole Algerian division to capture it from a handful of our men. It cost them a great number of dead – and equipment.'

'But it does cover the Cassino position, does it not, Field Marshal?' Jodl remarked quietly, speaking for the first time.

'One might say that,' Kesselring mumbled. 'But Cassino will hold even with Peak 555 lost. It is the lynch-pin of our line, and virtually impregnable,' his voice rose proudly, as if he personally were responsible for the creation of the mountain chain, which barred the Allies' progress north.

'Even if the Allies landed on the coast *behind* it?' Jodl persisted, playing the gadfly as usual, eager to provoke the self-important field commanders who came to the Führer's HQ full of themselves and the infallibility of their plans. Hitler held up his hand for peace.

'Please, gentlemen, let us not go into that now. We shall face that possibility when it occurs. For the time being, let us look at the Cassino situation. Kesselring, tell me a little more about it, please.'

Glad to have had Jodl silenced, Kesselring continued:

'It rises to five hundred and nineteen metres, my Führer, and commands the Liri valley to the south, the town of Cassino to the east and the Rapido valley running northwards towards S. Elia. It must be taken if the Allies are to use Route Six. On and around the Cassino position, we have the best troops available, the paratroop division – Heilmann's – and the Hermann Goering Panzer Grenadier Division, plus Colonel Geier's SS Battle Group Wotan in reserve.'

Hitler's face lit up.

'Did you hear that, Jodl? Geier's roughnecks from the SS are there too!'

Jodl pulled a long face.

'Yes, I heard, my Führer,' he said sourly. He knew the

THE CASSINO FRONT – WINTER 1943/44

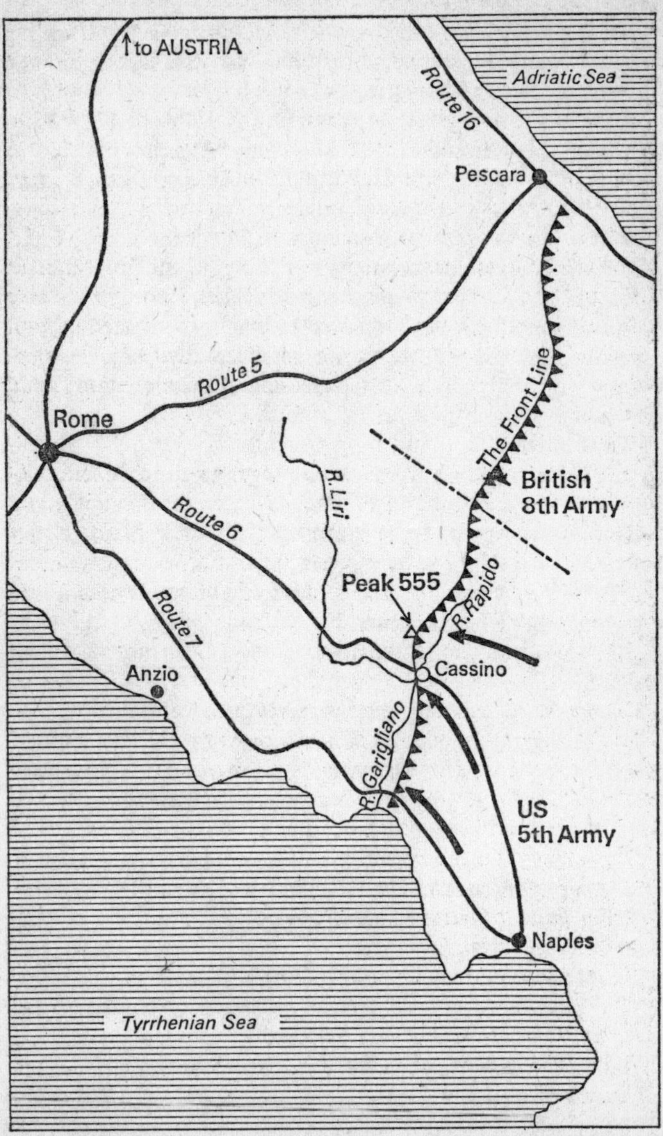

small ex-cavalryman Geier – the 'Vulture' as he was nick-named behind his back – well enough. Since 1939 he had had his battalion decimated time and time again on every battle-front in the ambitious drive for promotion. Admittedly Geier's SS Battlegroup was probably the best fighting unit on any front this winter of 1943 when the steam was running out of even the most elite outfits. But that quality had been purchased at a terrible price in blood and human suffering.

Neither the Führer nor 'Smiling Albert' noticed his look, however. Kesselring eagerly hurried on with his exposé:

'Our people are exceedingly well dug in, my Führer, and the Ami bombardment is largely ineffective. Their shelters are reinforced with steel and concrete so that they can get on with their business without interference from the enemy. Even when the bombers come in, they can safely sit there and play *Skat*.'*

Hitler smiled.

'We did the same in the Bavarian infantry in the trenches in the first war against the Tommies,' he remarked. 'Good, Kesselring. You seem to have everything very well under control. Now, I should like to make a suggestion. I want some of your paratroopers out of the bunkers and into the area of the monastery itself.'

Kesselring's mouth dropped open with shock, as Hitler had expected it would. The German Leader flashed a look at Jodl. Jodl was watching the Field Marshal, his eyes full of undisguised cynical pleasure. As a devout Roman Catholic, Kesselring had consistently leaned over backwards not to offend the Italian Church; Jodl knew what he must be thinking at this moment.

'But, my Führer,' he stuttered. 'The monastery – you know, of course, we have assured the Church authorities that nothing would happen to it during the course of the fighting?'

Hitler sighed wearily.

'It has been our misfortune, Kesselring, that we have the wrong religion.'

Kesselring flushed, but said nothing.

'Why couldn't we have had the Japanese religion which

* Popular Germany Army card game (*transl.*).

regards sacrifice for the Fatherland as the highest good? Why must we have Christianity with all that damned meekness and flabbiness? But we have and so do our enemies – and our friends, *Christian* France and Spain. Now the point is this, Kesselring. A great change is taking place in the course of the war. The days of 1940 and 1941 are over – for the time being. Unfortunately we Germans cannot do as we wish, without considering the attitudes and feelings of the rest of the world. We must take such things into account now and play their foolish Christian games. We must attempt to win the hearts of our potential allies – the neutrals. Do you understand?'

'Yes, my Führer.'

'Good, then you must realize that we vitally need a propaganda victory this winter. We must show the neutrals that we are not barbarians, as the enemy propaganda makes us out to be, but the defenders of the true faith.' He smiled cynically at the devout Field Marshal. 'Which we are, are we not?'

'Yes, yes,' Kesselring agreed hastily.

'There are also those enemies within our own ranks,' Hitler's face darkened, 'who must be rendered impotent by such a propaganda victory – in due course, the Gestapo will take care of them properly. But for the time being, we must be content with taking the wind out of their sails—'

'But Cassino?' Kesselring was provoked into interrupting. 'The connection with Cassino?'

'I was coming to that, my dear Field Marshal. Now what if the Allies thought we were using the monastery as an observation point?'

'But we aren't, my Führer!'

'Yes, but if *they* thought we were?'

'They would attempt to destroy the position – perhaps.'

'Perhaps. But because of the monastery's valuable antiquities, its venerability,' Hitler sneered, his contempt naked now, 'they might hesitate, eh?'

'Yes,' Kesselring conceded lamely.

'But if we provoked them into destroying that supposed observation post, Kesselring, and thus brought down the wrath of the so-called Christian world on their guilty heads?'

'How, sir? We haven't the strength for any large-scale operation. The front is at a stalemate. As Jodl has indicated they are probably at this moment gathering their strength for an amphibious landing behind the Cassino position, somewhere higher up the coast. If that comes off, Cassino will lose in importance. There will be no need to – neutralize,' he coughed over the word, as if he could not bring himself to utter the word 'destroy' – 'the Cassino line.'

Politely Hitler let him finish.

'All very sound reasoning, Kesselring. But you are forgetting one thing.'

'And that is, my Führer?'

'Colonel Geier's SS Battle Group Wotan!' Hitler snapped, iron in his voice. 'We shall use his roughnecks to provoke the Allies into destroying that precious monastery of yours. Kesselring, I want you to give an immediate order to Tenth Army Commander that Colonel Geier's men recapture Peak 555.'

THREE

Major von Dodenburg's eyes were beginning to get used to the darkness now. As the long attack column from the Wotan's Panzer Grenadier Battalion came closer to their start line, he was able to pick out the trenches abandoned by the original German defenders of Peak 555 when the French had struck them with such overwhelming weight. Here and there he could make out their dead, strung across the barbed wire like rag dolls.

Behind him Schulze, the battalion's comedian from Hamburg, cursed softly and tugged at the mule's bridle.

'Come on you bitch, move!'

'What's the matter, Schulze?' he hissed at the man who had been with him now since the earliest days of the Wotan SS Assault Battalion.

'It's these mules, sir,' Schulze answered in his Waterfront sing-song. 'You toss a coin and takes yer choice – heads the bastards take a lump out of yer arse, tails, they kick it.'

He tugged at the obstinate little animal again, whose hooves were muffled in sacking to cut down the noise.

'All right,' von Dodenburg whispered, grinning. 'You've registered your protest, but keep the noise down. They tell me those Africans up there have sharp ears.'

'Yeah, and sharp knives too,' Schulze said dourly. 'Those Goums cut the tails off a couple of paras last week and when a patrol found them, they had their tails stuck in their traps.'

'Can't worry you, Schulze,' the handsome young SS Major commented, waving his hand for the column to continue up the steep, treacherous track. 'The way you've been abusing yours, it must have fallen off years ago.'

Behind them in the darkness, the tough, rangy South Tyrolean farmboys who made up most of the First Company laughed softly and urged on their commandeered Italian mules, which carried the ammunition and rations they would need once they had captured the Peak and had dug in.

They plodded on carefully, bodies held tense and expectant, waiting for the sudden dramatic hush of a flare which would indicate that they had been discovered by the French. But none came. As a thick cold mist began to roll down from the peak, they started to work their way through the abandoned trenches. Once von Dodenburg stopped and glanced down at a dead paratrooper, sprawled on his back, his legs spread apart, his jump-suit ripped open down the middle. Where his genitals had once been, there was now nothing but a bloody mess. Schulze's story had not been another of his macabre inventions. Von Dodenburg swallowed hard and straightening up hastily, urged the grenadiers on before they could get a proper look at the para's mutilated body.

They passed between two miserable white-painted Italian cottages, their pathetic little gardens, littered with French and German equipment, both roofs gone. Kuno von Dodenburg, followed by Schulze carrying his Schmeisser machine pistol, gave them a quick examination. But they backed out hastily. They stank rankly of poverty, animals and human excreta – and in the second one, an old Italian woman lay huddled in a corner, one shoe gone, her black skirt thrown up over her head to reveal the obscenely naked flesh beneath.

'The Frogs don't think much of putting out sentries, do they sir?' Schulze said after a while, as they left the huts behind them.

'No, obviously not,' von Dodenburg answered softly, still trying to absorb the discovery of the mutilated para and the raped Italian crone. 'They're too confident they have beaten us for good, it seems.'

He glanced up at the stark black outline of the peak far above, towering up through the grey cold mist.

'Wotan will teach them to be more careful next time, won't it, Schulze?'

'If you say so, sir,' Schulze answered non-committally.

They plodded on.

Four hours later the sentries did not have to wake them in the miserable holes they had scraped in the iron-hard earth, ready for the dawn stand-to. The mist that covered the mountain side was freezing cold and most of them lay in their camouflaged capes, awake and shivering.

Stiff-legged and shuddering, Major von Dodenburg crossed over to the battalion HQ, a hole covered by four camouflaged capes, clipped together to hide the light of the lantern. Here and there a trooper was attempting to wash himself from the water in his canteen; but most of them were standing around in a daze, munching mechanically on slices of hard Army bread or urinating on the naked rock. As he passed the mule lines, Schulze got up sleepily from where he had been bedding down between two of the animals and gave him a parody of a salute.

'Well, I must admit the bastards keep you warm,' he said thickly. 'But both of them snored worse than a couple of drunken whores!'

Von Dodenburg grinned and pushing open the flap of the cape, dropped inside. The radio operator, bent over his set in the yellow glow of the lantern turned, startled.

'It's only me,' the CO said. 'And if it had been one of those Goums, it would have been too late anyway. They would have slit your throat – or worse by now ... All right, what's the situation?'

Quickly Major von Dodenburg set about putting his battalion in order for the attack. In less than sixty minutes, the barrage would begin and as soon as it ended, his first two companies, scattered all over the western side of the Peak, would have to be ready to move in. He'd seen often enough what happened to infantry when they waited too long to move in after the softening-up shelling had finished. He would start moving his first two companies in immediately, chancing a few casualties from shorts or delayed action fuses.

Some time later Schulze came in and thrust a canteen cup at him.

'Here, drink that,' he commanded. 'Cold nigger sweat' – he meant Army coffee – 'and a good shot of *grappa*.'

'That's not the way to talk to your commanding officer,' he said without rancour and accepted the cup.

'It's the tin, sir,' Schulze said. 'Gives me special privileges, you see. Only common soldier in the Battle Group with the throatache.'

He tapped the black-and-white metal of the Knight's Cross of the Iron Cross which hung from his neck significantly.

Von Dodenburg took a swig of the fiery Italian spirit and gasped.

'Yes, Schulze, and one of these days that big Hamburg mouth of yours is going to get you a nice old arse-ache too. But thanks all the same.'

Schulze sniffed. 'After four years in the Wotan, what could happen to me that—'

'You might have to face me, Schulze,' a well-known Prussian voice rasped coldly, and Colonel Geier – the Vulture – Wotan's monocled CO dropped lightly into the hole, armed as usual only with his riding crop.

'*Achtung!*' von Dodenburg snapped and tried to come to attention in the confined space.

'None of that foolishness, von Dodenburg! We are not playing soldiers now.' As Captain Schwarz, his one-armed adjutant, dropped into the hole, the Vulture pushed by Schulze to the map. 'Everything in order?' he asked, looking down at it, his monstrous beak of a nose which had helped to give him his nickname silhouetted in the yellow light.

'Yessir. H-hour is at zero six hours. My two lead companies will jump off at zero six, ten. Companies three and four will follow at a two hundred metres interval. I shall go in with the third company.'

'Good.' The Vulture looked up, screwing his monocle more firmly in his cold blue eye. 'I think we shall catch them on the hop. If there's any trouble, I've got the tank battalion dismounted and ready to give you additional support. I shall go up with you, however. Schwarz here will maintain contact.'

Schwarz's crazy eyes flashed a look of acknowledgement.

'It could be dangerous, sir,' von Dodenburg said a little hesitantly, afraid of provoking one of the Vulture's unpredictable rages.

'I know, von Dodenburg, and I can assure you that I treasure my skin as much as the next man. But as you know the operation has been ordered by the Führer himself and if I am to obtain those precious general's stars, I must ensure that the greatest captain of all times is not disappointed, eh?'

He grinned cynically as he used the malicious term for the Führer. Schwarz, the fanatical National Socialist, whose uncle. murdered by British killers the previous summer, had been the great Heydrich himself, glared at the CO. Von Dodenburg contented himself with a faint shake of his head. The Vulture had absolutely no feeling whatsoever for the National Socialist cause; his sole concern was promotion and more promotion, indeed that was why the ex-regular cavalryman had transferred to Himmler's Black Guards in the first place. Promotion was quicker in the elite SS formation. But there was no time now to waste on such considerations. H-hour was approaching rapidly.

'I suggest we go out now, sir,' he said, throwing a quick glance at his watch. 'The lead companies will already be forming up.'

'Good,' the Vulture said. 'Schwarz, take over here. I shall dispense with my bodyguards. Use them to throw out a picket line. Anyone coming down from the peak unwounded or not on orders, shoot them'!

'But sir,' von Dodenburg protested, his pale face flushing hotly. 'My men—'

'Your men are like the rest these days, von Dodenburg.' The Vulture cut him short. 'The steam is going out of our dear stubble-hoppers, even if they do belong to the SS. We must ensure that they understand we won't allow them to lose that steam. Come on!' Gripping his cane more firmly, he swung himself out of the hole with easy grace.

Outside the two leading companies were already formed up in two well-spaced out lines, disappearing into the grey mist on both sides. Here and there men fiddled with their equipment or munched bars of chocolate, slowly becoming high on the drug pervitin which they contained; but for the most part they crouched tensely, their eyes fixed on the peak which stood out above the mist.

The Vulture gave them a hard look and then turned to the remaining two companies, still in their foxholes and in some cases digging them even deeper. They were the veterans. They knew the enemy counterfire would start hitting their lines, once the Frogs had recovered from the shock of the initial artillery barrage; they were not going to be caught out in the open. The Vulture nodded his approval.

'Everything seems to be in best butter, von Dodenburg,' he snapped, using the soldiers' phrase and slapping his cane against the side of his polished cavalry boots. 'Let us go over and join the second line.'

Von Dodenburg indicated that Schulze, who was to act as his bodyguard during the attack, should follow and together they stumbled over the rough, mist-shrouded hillside to the waiting SS men. The attack could begin.

It did so with a frightening, earth-shaking roar. At the stroke of six, the whole of the Hermann Goering Division artillery crashed into action. With a hoarse exultant scream the heavy shells tore over their heads. Flight after flight of hushing fiery rockets flew after them from the multiple electric mortars, ripping the still dawn apart in savage fury. The first angry sighs became a baleful howl. It mounted in intensity, elemental yet controlled. It grew to become a monstrous Wagnerian cocophony.

The first French line of defence disappeared. The shells moved on to the second one, their explosions splitting the mist apart in ugly red spurts of flame. To the right of the peak something began to burn suddenly. Perhaps a fuel dump. Still the artillery kept up its terrible inhuman hammering. Surely no one could live through it, Kuno von Dodenburg told himself, eyeing the tense faces of his men, coloured a sickly red hue by the flames from the French dump. But he knew there would be some who would survive; there always were.

And then as abruptly as it had started, the barrage stopped, leaving an echoing silence behind it, which reverberated back and forth from the amphitheatre of the surrounding peaks.

The next instant the officers of the first two companies were on their feet, waving their arms and blowing their whistles urgently. The NCOs followed, yelling at the troopers and pushing them forward with their machine pistols. Somewhere a slow French machine gun began to chatter like an angry woodpecker. The troopers, their rifles held across their chests protectively, stumbled on up the hill. The French reacted quickly. There was a sudden series of obscene plops. A salvo of mortar bombs straddled the waiting men. Huge holes appeared suddenly among their ranks.

'*Stretcher-bearer!*' a thin voice screamed hysterically.

'*Stand fast!*' von Dodenburg yelled instantly, springing to his feet, as red-hot, razor-sharp slivers of metal hissed through the air around them.

Above them there was the crackle of small arms fire. The attackers responded. The Schmeissers returned the fire with hysterical, high-pitched urgency. Tracer stitched white and red patterns through the mist. There were long answering bursts from the slower French machine guns. Von Dodenburg bit his lip and flung an urgent glance at the green glowing dial of his wrist-watch. Nearly time to move off.

'I'll piss up my sleeve, sir, but you're going to get yourself killed standing up like that!' Schulze screamed above the din.

'Shut up, Schulze!' von Dodenburg yelled.

The first casualties began stumbling back down the hillside. As they came through the line of NCOs set up by Schwarz, the waiting men could see their eyes were wild with shock. Mumbling meaningless phrases, raising their bloodied arms they jogged on towards the aid station below.

Von Dodenburg placed his whistle between his teeth. A bareheaded trooper, his arms flailing wildly, his weapon gone, came blundering through their lines. The Vulture sprang up. He thrust his cane neatly between the panic-stricken boy's legs. He crashed full length in the dirt, and lay there gasping wildly. As von Dodenburg blew the first blast on his whistle, the Vulture yelled:

'Schwarz, over here! . . . A deserter . . . Shoot the bastard at once!'

'*Follow me!*' von Dodenburg bellowed.

The Third and Fourth Companies obeyed immediately. They knew it was safer to move forward than to stay where they were. They rose at once.

'*Alles fuer Deutschland!*' von Dodenburg screamed the motto of the SS.

'*Alles fuer Deutschland!*' four hundred throats took up the cry, as they surged forward.

Within minutes the two companies were broken up into little groups of men, jumping from hole to hole, dropping suddenly in gasping panic as white streams of tracer cut the air at waist-height and stumbling to their feet again under the blows and kicks of their officers and NCOs. Now they began suffering casualties. Somewhere to their right a nest of slow-firing French machine-guns cut great swathes through their ranks, flinging men right and left like puppets.

'Grenades – heaven, arse and twine, man!' the Vulture gasped, 'give me your grenades, Schulze.'

The big Hamburger pulled the two stick grenades from his belt.

Hastily the Vulture thrust his cane down the side of his boot.

'Carry on, von Dodenburg, I'll see to those damned Frog guns!'

With unusual speed for such an old man, he doubled off in the direction of the French machine-gun nest.

Von Dodenburg and the little group of men with him hurried forward, dodging a shell which filled the air with hissing red-hot shards. A dark face loomed up out of the night. At first von Dodenburg took it to be that of one of his own men, with his face blackened. Then he saw the man's thick lips. A Sengalese!

The French colonial soldier reacted slowly. Von Dodenburg did not give him a chance to recover. He fired a burst from the hip. At that range the 9mm slugs ripped the man almost in half. The Sengalese's knees gave way and he began to sink to the ground. Von Dodenburg kicked him in the face. Just in time. Another soldier was coming at him with a bayonet. Before the German officer could fire, the Negro lunged. The bayonet sliced along his hand. He felt the hot blood spurt over his knuckles suddenly. He yelped with pain. The next instant Schulze ripped off an angry burst. The Negro was bowled over screaming piteously.

They ran on, zig-zagging between the shell bursts, springing over the sudden holes. From behind came the crump of Schulze's potato mashers. The Vulture had successfully put the

French machine-gun nest out of action! The troopers it had pinned down came rushing up to join the confused attack, screaming with rage at the horror and misery of it all. Von Dodenburg blew his whistle shrilly.

'*To me – to me, Wotan!*' he yelled desperately and spread his fingers on the top of his helmet in the infantry sign for rally.

They ran towards him, their rifles tossed to one side, their sweating hands gripping axes, knives, bayonets – anything that would cut and hack and allow them to work off their animal fury.

'Forward!' von Dodenburg commanded and firing a wild burst from the hip, lead the charge.

Scrambling over the dead and dying of the first wave, they slammed into the Sengalese line. Like a pack of wild animals, they began the terrible work of slaughter, slashing, hacking, slicing, gouging without mercy.

A white officer loomed up out of the mist, a revolver in his hand. Von Dodenburg squeezed the trigger of his machine-pistol. Nothing happened. The Frenchman raised his pistol. Von Dodenburg could see his face contorted with absolute terror. In a paroxysm of fear, he brought up the Schmeisser's steel butt. It caught the Frenchman under the chin. He screamed. A clot of blood shot out of the side of his mouth. His head flew back, neck broken. As he crumpled another trooper kicked him in the face.

But von Dodenburg did not have time to look. The Sengalese were everywhere. His hands shaking badly, von Dodenburg tried to fit another magazine to his machine-pistol. He failed miserably. With a curse he flung the mp away and pulled out his pistol.

'*Oh, les salauds!*' he heard someone curse close by in the fog.

He turned and fired instinctively. There was a scream of agony as a big Negro sergeant clutched his chest and dropped. Behind him his companion gave a cry of rage in a language von Dodenburg could not understand and charged at the German officer with a unwieldly, old-fashioned bayonet. He did not get far.

Schulze popped up from somewhere or other. Von Dodenburg caught a glimpse of the Reeperbahn equalizer Schulze wore on his right hand. A moment later the brass knuckles, propelled by the full strength of his docker's muscles, smashed into the Negro's face. The man staggered back as if he had just run into a brick wall. The rifle fell from his nerveless fingers. His knees began to sag. But Schulze didn't give him a chance. He brought up his big knee cruelly. It crashed into the Sengalese's crotch. His scream was stifled with vomit and he flew backwards, howling like an animal and grabbing frantically at his genitals.

A single, slow-firing machine-gun barred their way from behind a ruined wall. In front of it were the heaped dead of the first wave. Whoever was manning it was a veteran. He kept sweeping a slow arc of thirty degrees regularly, the red tracer cutting through the darkness like a swarm of angry hornets.

'Flanks – for God's sake to the flanks!' von Dodenburg yelled desperately.

The troopers spread out at last. Von Dodenburg picked up an abandoned assault rifle and poured a stream of lead at the gunner. He reacted at once. The fiery tracer hissed towards him. He ducked hastily. His nostrils were suddenly full of the burnt smell of tracer as stone chips flew all around him.

Then the men on the flanks went in. The gunner swung his machine-gun round. Too late! A parcel of stick grenades hurtled through the air. The gun exploded in a burst of ugly yellow-red flame. The next instant von Dodenburg was up and running forward again. As he sprang over the ruined wall, he caught a glimpse of the dead French gunner sprawled across his shattered gun. Headless.

Five minutes later the French resistance broke. Just ahead of von Dodenburg a gigantic Sengalese threw away his rifle and yelled in a thick slurred bass, '*sauve qui peut!*' But although the cry was almost unintelligible, his comrades understood it well enough.

'*Shof ki po!*' they cried to one another in absolute panic.

A white officer sprang to his feet in full view of the attacking SS men and screamed at them:

'*Cochons . . . salauds . . . restez là!*' He attempted to spread out his hands to stop them. But they jumped from their positions, throwing away their rifles, and swept by him.

The next moment a German bullet struck him in the chest and he fell to the ground. In their panic the Negroes ran over him, pressing the dying officer deeper and deeper into the blood-red mire. Now they had no other thought but to escape from the murderous German fire. Frantically they fought each other to escape, that animal cry of utter fear following them as they fled down the other side of the mountain!

'Shof ki po . . . shof ki po . . .'

As the pale winter sun rose above the mountain and the majestic white-capped peak, towering above the exhausted SS men below, came into view, shedding the night mist, the panting, bleeding victors stared at the heap of churned-up rubble for which they had fought and, in some cases, died that night. Everywhere there were bodies, sprawled out in the extravagant postures of the dead: their own and those of the Goums, lean dark men, with cropped hair save for a pigtail which Allah was supposed to grab to haul them to Paradise at the moment of death. But Allah had apparently failed them, von Dodenburg, his chest still heaving hectically, told himself cynically. Their corpses were mingled with those of their heathen Sengalese comrades, firmly rooted on the bloody earth. Gods, Christian or otherwise, seemed to keep their noses out of violent action, preferring the bourgeois peace of the churches.

He sighed and raising his helmet wiped the sweat from his brow. Despite the dawn cold, he was sweating all over. He walked over to a group of his own men from the First Company who had been caught by a burst of French machine-gun fire. Even in death, their last feverish gestures of devotion to duty were apparent in their postures: one, his hand arrested in mid-air, as if he were about to pull the stick grenade out of his belt and throw it; another killed in the act of changing a magazine in his Schmeisser; yet another, his body arched backwards slightly, an almost triumphant look on his waxen face, as he reached for his pistol to finish off some unsuspecting Negro.

'Sir,' Schulze's voice cut into his reverie.

He swung round. The big Hamburger still wore his

'Reeperbahn equalizer', a dull gleam of blood on the brass knuckles. In his other hand, he had a cheap metal wristwatch and a big thick bundle of French franc notes.

'Finding things before they're lost again, eh, Schulze?' he asked wearily, slinging the assault rifle over his shoulder.

'The stiffs won't be needing them no more, sir, will they?' Schulze said with a big grin. 'Stands to reason. Besides I bet they wouldn't object to me having a little bit of the other on the strength of their Marie.* Solidarity of the working classes, you know.'

'Go on, you Bolshevik, you! God knows how you've kept out of the Gestapo's hands so long. I certainly don't.'

'Just my handsome mug and my natural charm, sir – that's all.' He thrust the looted money in his back pocket. 'Colonel Geier asks if you would walk across to his C.P. They've got a prisoner there – an Ami.'

'An Ami?'

Von Dodenburg whistled through his teeth. In his four years of war the young officer had only fought against the Americans once; but it had been a brief skirmish and they had not taken any prisoners.

'Yes, sir, a citizen of the land of boundless possibilities,' Schulze said, using the contemptuous term for America. 'And I think he's going to do it in his pants before the Colonel is finished with him.'

But for once the big Hamburger was wrong. The American liaison officer with the French Algerian Division was apparently unaffected by the fact that he was prisoner-of-war now and in the hands of a unit which reputedly did not take prisoners, or if they did inadvertantly, ensured that they were 'shot while attempting to escape' on their way back to the cages. Squatting on the ground at Geier's feet, chewing gum while Schwarz interpreted his words, he seemed completely resigned to his fate with a certain cynical nonchalance which von Dodenburg could not help admiring.

'It was going to be one of the great marches in all military history,' he said without any trace of rancour on his lean handsome face. 'In Africa they told us, we would march up this

* Soldiers' slang for money (*transl.*).

beautiful country, filled with beautiful people, and be welcomed like Hollywood film stars all the way. Of course, we fellahs from the 36th Division are Texans and we kinda believe tall tales. But all the same the thing had a ring of truth about it. A handsome people, eager to be liberated, the dago red flowing like water and all those Eyetie dames.' The captured Ami kissed his fingers in what von Dodenburg couldn't help thinking was a very un-American gesture. '*Brother!*'

His cynical grin vanished and his lean face grew harder.

'That's what they said anyhow. Roses, roses all the way – and what did we get? We got this!' He spread out his hand at the scene of destruction all around him. 'Colder than a well digger's ass up here and not exactly what I'd call a hidyho Texas welcome, Colonel!' He looked up directly at the Vulture, who was staring at him, as if he were a visitor from another planet.

'Do you think we can get anything else from him, Schwarz?' Colonel Geier rasped. 'The American 36th Division in liaison with the French Algerian – so it means we've got the US Second Corps facing us down there.' He indicated the plain below, still shrouded with the December fog. 'Could he tell us any more?'

Schwarz shook his head.

'No, sir. The man's a fool. It's obvious – just another Texan cowboy, that's all.'

The Vulture gave von Dodenburg an inquiring look. The young Major indicated he had no questions to ask.

'All right, Schwarz, would you take care of him, please?' the Vulture snapped. 'Von Dodenburg come with me please.'

The American officer's lean face paled a little, but if he knew what was coming, he gave no sign of it. Obediently he let himself be led away by the one-armed Captain.

'Roses, roses all the way – that's what they said,' he muttered, as they disappeared behind one of the shattered walls. 'And we believed it.'

A moment later a single shot rang out, and Schwarz came back alone.

FOUR

'Oh, those goddam Frogs,' the tall craggy-faced commander of the US Fifth Army groaned when he had read the message. 'Why the hell does everyone always let me down in this command?' He jerked his head up and looked accusingly at the assembled brass from the Second Corps. 'What the Sam Hill were the Frogs doing up there on that mountain – getting in some sack time?'

Captain Pearson, General Clark's aide, who had brought the message in, recognized the signs. The Commander of the Fifth Army took anything which stopped or hindered the race up Italy towards the prize of Rome as a personal insult. His colossal vanity made him think that everyone was out to sabotage his chances of becoming the head of the US Army one day.

'No, sir general,' he said boldly, feeling sorry for the French who had to fight, using the cast-offs of the British and American Armies. 'They were alert – in fact they were standing to when the Ted hit them.* But there was a thick mist at the time—'

The Commanding General turned from the window and strode across the farmhouse kitchen which served as the Second Corps HQ, bending his head to avoid hitting the ring of garlic hanging from the low beam.

'Don't give me that, Pearson,' he snapped, 'I know the Frogs. I served with them in France in the First War – and I've goddam seen enough of them in this war in North Africa. They let me down then and they've let me down again now.' He shook his head in disgust and stared down at the map of the front spread out on what had once been a kitchen table. 'A goddam lot of YBSOBs!' He spelled out the letters of his favourite curse – 'Yellow-bellied sons-of-bitches' with relish.

For a few moments there was no sound in the little Italian farmhouse. Outside there was the steady rumble of the heavy

* Army slang for the *Tedeschi*, i.e. 'Germans' (*transl.*).

guns, the constant background music of war, and the dry cough of a jeep's motor being turned over and failing to start in the icy cold. Then General Walker, the stocky commander of the 36th Infantry Division, said:

'Don't take it to heart, sir. Put it down to a bit of bad luck, eh?'

Fred Walker had once been Clark's instructor at the War College and he felt he could talk to the tall rangy Army commander in a more familiar manner than most of the other Second Corps brass. On this icy December day, however, he was wrong – badly wrong. Clark swung round on him.

'Bad luck, eh? *Bad luck* is all I ever hear in my command! One goddam piece of bad luck after another, staring at Salerno, Fred. I guess that was bad luck too, eh!'

General Walker flushed and bit his lower lip to hold back his angry retort. Pearson, watching the exchange, felt for Walker. His Thirty-Six, a Texan National Guard outfit, was a hell of a mess. Not only were Walker's senior officers hopelessly incompetent, but the Regular Army man had indulged in a couple of bad cases of nepotism, appointing two of his own sons to high staff positions. The young aide knew that there were plenty of people on Clark's own staff who breathed a sigh of relief every time the Texans went out of the line, feeling that there at least they couldn't cause trouble.

'The 36th have had a hard row to hoe, General,' Keyes, the Corps Commander intervened hastily. 'It seems that Fred's doggies always get the hind tit.'

'Maybe – maybe,' Clark said, staring down at the map again for a moment, as if he were trying to discover something there which was being hidden from his gaze purposely.

'I don't understand the Krauts, gentlemen,' he said, looking up again, his craggy face creased in bewilderment. 'Intelligence says they're strapped for bodies, yet they pull off a humdinger of an attack this morning. Was that thing on Peak 555 just a local attack? Or are they testing our strength in the Liri Valley prior to pulling off a major attack at the same time when we land?'

'You mean at Anzio, sir?' Keyes asked in alarm.

'Of course, I damn well do!' Clark snapped. 'Where else?

What if when we go in at Anzio, they come down from that goddam peak and really lam into us? We'll be weakened by two divisions taking part in the Anzio landing as it is. Boy, they'd really catch us with our skivvies down.'

He paused and looked round the faces of the assembled brass threateningly.

'And I'd like you to remember if they did, all your heads would roll. I don't intend to be the fall guy like Eisenhower almost was at the Kasserine Pass. You understand that, don't you?' he added, lowering his voice so that they got the full significance of his threat.

'Yes, General,' they mumbled.

Pearson, watching the little scene, thanked God once again that he was not a regular officer, but an 'eighty-day wonder', in the Army for the duration of the war only. How often in these past nine months had he seen senior officers, whose orders could mean life or death for thousands of men, eat crow like this, all for the sake of advancement.

'All right, gentlemen, what are we going to do?' Clark's voice rose again. '*This* is what we're gonna do! It's bad enough with those YBSOBs on Cassino staring down our throats every time we open 'em to yell chow. But I'm not going to tolerate the Krauts holding that Peak, ready to jump us down here whenever the hell they damn well please. Geoffrey,' he addressed Keyes, 'I'm going to take out Peak 555 with your guys.'

Keyes absorbed the information in silence. Clark, he knew, would tell him what to do as usual; the Army Commander was not in business for suggestions at this particular moment.

'I recommend you use Fred's 36th for the job.'

'But, General,' Walker protested. 'My boys are scheduled for the crossing of the Rapido. I need all strength available for that. If I fritter my men away—' he shrugged, leaving the sentence unfinished.

'I know, Fred. After all I am the Army Commander,' Clark said with barely concealed sarcasm.

'May I make a suggestion, sir?' It was Colonel Porter, the soft-spoken second corps Deputy Chief-of-Staff, who Pearson thought looked more like a Mid-Western high school principal than a professional soldier.

'What is it, Bob?' Clark asked.

'Why not use the 93rd Regiment attached at the moment to General Walker's division?'

'*The black boys!*' someone among the brass exclaimed in surprise.

'Yes,' Walker said emphatically. 'They've been up here four weeks now. They've got to go into action some time. We're strapped for men and even if they are relatively inexperienced, they outnumber those Teds up there three to one at least.'

Clark hesitated. He was not a politically-minded man like Eisenhower or the limey Montgomery. But he did know enough of the situation in the USA to realize that America's first Negro combat regiment was a political issue, especially as the War Department had made so much publicity about them, plastering the front pages of papers all over the States with pictures of coloured master and staff sergeants in the supply services, sacrificing their rank to become PFCs in a combat outfit.

'What do you think, Fred?' he asked at last.

Walker hesitated.

'Well, General, they're as ready as they're ever gonna be. But I don't know.' He bit his lip. 'Hell, you know me – I command a Texan division and those buckos of mine don't like black boys. They don't even like white guys – if they don't come from Texas!'

There was a burst of laughter from the rest of the brass, hastily suppressed when they saw the look on Clark's face.

'What about you, Geoffrey?'

Keyes was a much smarter man than Walker. At that moment, Pearson could see the Corps Commander's mind racing, trying to outguess the big Commanding General. Did Clark want the Negroes to carry out the attack or not? That was the problem. And in the end Keyes solved it in the manner that Pearson had come to expect from those senior officers who were going to survive the course. He compromised.

'Well, sir,' he said, 'Bob here and Fred say that the 93rd are trained and, after all they are volunteers, even their white officers. So their spirit should make up for their other defects. In addition they outnumber the Krauts, as Fred has pointed out. So I say, let them have a crack at taking out the Peak.' He shrugged. 'And if they don't pull it off, at least they'll have worn the Krauts down and we can still send in Fred's Texans.'

'Good,' Clark picked up his cap with its outsize lieutenant-general's stars and nodded to Pearson to follow him, 'then that's that. The black boys will do it.'

With Clark in the lead, the brass streamed out into the winter morning. The white helmeted MPs of his escort snapped to attention and the correspondents and cameramen surged forward, shouting questions and levelling their cameras to get a shot of Clark. As usual, the Fifth Army's Commanding General was more than approachable. Pearson grinned, as he turned his face so that the cameramen could photograph his left side – his best – and answered the correspondents' yelled demands for information with his conceit wrapped round him like a halo.

'Just say, gentlemen,' he bellowed above the racket, 'that General Mark Clark's Fifth Army has got the situation well in hand. And off the cuff – so don't quote me on this, gentlemen – you can expect to hear that Peak 555 is back in the possession of General Mark Clark's Fifth Army within the next seven days. Okay, Pearson, let's get the hell out of here. It's colder than a well-digger's ass.'

The brass snapped to attention and the jeep shot away, followed by the outrider escort of MPs on their gleaming motor cycles.

The staff of the US Second Corps relaxed. Their hands came down from the gleaming lacquered helmets, with the silver and gold insignia. Someone broke wind. A colonel spat into the mud of the farmyard. Slowly they began to drift back into the farmhouse HQ.

'Waal,' the big Colonel who had spat, said to his neighbour in a thick Alabaman voice, heavy with whisky and a lifetime of prejudice, 'it sure looks as if those niggers are gonna get their asses well and truly licked, don't it?' He hawked and spat again.

FIVE

On the same morning that General Mark Clark visited the Second Corps, the Vulture gave the assembled officers of his Battle Group Wotan a little lecture.

Standing in front of the new command post which he had set up between two prominent hillocks that Schulze had already nicknamed Twin Tits, he rasped:

'Gentlemen, this is where we are going to stand. I have no further orders from Smiling Albert' – he allowed himself a cold little smile at the nickname – 'than these – stand and fight!'

He flung out his hand in an expansive gesture and the assembled SS officers stared around at the barren mountain top, covered in the debris of war, which seemed such an offence to the noble dignity of the snow-capped peak towering above them.

'In essence, gentlemen, we have an area of four square kilometres to defend and some fourteen hundred men to do it with? Now, I don't need to tell you that that is not a very large number of bodies. So what are we going to do?'

He paused, tugged at the end of his monstrous nose which had turned salmon pink in the biting cold.

'We must make this peak so costly to the Amis down there in the valley that they will give up in the end. Every man in this battle group who dies – and there will be plenty, you can be sure of that – must take six Amis with him. But as you can fully appreciate, we cannot do this if we do not make the most of the natural defences of this place.'

He pointed his riding crop at a couple of the lanky Tyroleans idly scratching at the frozen rock a few metres away.

'Not like that, of course. Ground, as you all know from your studies at Bad Toelz and since, is the raw material of the soldier, just as his weapons are his tools. A foolish inexperienced soldier does little with that raw material; an experienced solider shapes it exactly to his purpose. What then is the purpose of this peak which we now hold? At the moment it is simply an observation point. But is also an automatic target of attack by the enemy who not only wants to knock out this observation point, but also wants to use it for his own observation purposes. Thus, in modern warfare, the advance of an attacking army is from one piece of high ground to the next.'

Major von Dodenburg let his eyes wander over the sterile earth of the mountain top, pitted with shell holes and littered with jagged pieces of rusting shrapnel like the scabs of some ugly skin disease. His gaze passed over the slope, covered with belts of ammunition, abandoned weapons, grenades which had not exploded, rags of uniform, paper – plenty of paper – and here and there, crumpled bodies, on to the Liri Valley below. In spite of the haze, and to the left a man-made smoke screen, he could see the Allied lines quite clearly: silent, with no visible movement, but somehow sinister in their very silence.

'I have discovered in my years in the military,' the Vulture was saying, 'that the Army fits in well with a certain form of laziness. Army life is divided very equally between moments of hardship, fatigue, danger – and periods of inactivity. We had the former yesterday. Today – and every new day that dawns before the Amis attack – you gentlemen and your men are in for the latter.'

'What do you mean, sir?' Schwarz asked, always eager for an opportunity to inspire the cynical veterans of the Wotan with National Socialist purpose and enthusiasm.

'I mean, my dear Schwarz, that the men are going to dig, dig and dig yet more until they reach hell, as far as I am concerned.' The Vulture's voice rose harshly. 'Gentlemen we are going to turn Peak 555 into a fort that will never be taken. It will become a running sore for the Allies.' His hard blue eyes swept round their eager faces, glowing in the cold air. 'For if we don't stop the enemy here, gentlemen, Cassino over there will go, and with it the whole Winter Line. And if the Winter Line goes, we have lost Italy. The war will arrive then on the Reich's own doorstep and I don't have to tell you what that would mean to our hard-pressed homeland. *Meine Herren,* that is all!'

Schwarz, his black eyes gleaming fanatically, flung his arm up, as the rest snapped to attention.

'That will never happen, sir,' he barked eagerly. '*Sieg Heil!*'

'*Sieg Heil!*' the cry rose and reverberated around the mountain top, harsh, brutal and arrogant, flung out like a challenge to fate itself.

One hour later, the Wotan men began to transform Peak 555 into a fort. The ground was iron-hard, but a grenade buried in its surface soon softened it up so that the digging could commence. By the end of the first day, when the pale yellow ball of the winter snow started to slide behind the snow-covered peak, they had created a series of shallow holes all along the perimeter of the plateau below it. These were covered with sacking and rags which they had waterproofed with a mixture of rifle oil, paint, petrol and candle-wax. When the Americans still did not counter-attack on the following day, the hard work of digging commenced once more, the men burying into the Italian earth like moles. That evening their narrow one-man foxholes, each shaped like a coffin, were deep enough and they set about making them comfortable. As a sweating Schulze joked to von Dodenburg:

'They laughed when I started digging this.' He pointed to the hole, with its straw filled mattress at the base and the stove made from a twenty-litre French oil drum, already glowing invitingly. 'But now the joke's on them. You see there's nothing like a nice warm bed to come home to at night. Just stretch out your hands, sir and feel the warmth given out by that thing!'

'No thank you, Schulze, and I'm not going to ask where you stole the fuel from for it either, you rogue. Come on, out of there, I'm going to plant a spandau here. You'll cover my CP with it.'

Schulze wiped the sweat off his big red face with the back of his hand.

'All right, sir, I'm coming. But that's always the trouble with this shitty war – it breaks up a feller's home life!'

By the end of the third day, Battle Group Wotan was dug in and waiting for the enemy to appear. The Americans, hidden by the permanent smoke-screen below still did not come, and life on the Peak began to settle in to the routine of a military encampment.

Schulze, together with one of the ex-inmates of Torgau military prison, who had been conscripted into the Battle Group just after it had moved to the Italian front, made a crystal radio set from an empty cardboard GI ration container, copper wire taken from a shell and a couple of razor blades. And in the evening after stand-down, a group of the troopers would crowd round it, listening to American jazz from the Allied military station and frying potatoes in the howitzer recoil mechanism oil which Schulze had 'organized' somehow or other.

'They taste pretty good, sir,' Schulze told an amused von Dodenburg during the course of one of his evening rounds, 'but that oil gives yer a nice old case of the Cassino trots next morning – nearly takes the ring out of yer ass, it does!'

'I remember in Russia one time,' the ex-Torgau man said after von Dodenburg had gone, 'I was caught off-guard by a salvo from an Ivan Stalin Organ* and I jumped in this hole without thinking. I should have. The hole was full of crap!'

The Tyrolean boys laughed softly in the growing darkness, warming their frozen hands on the hot metal sides of their canteen cups full of bitter 'nigger sweat'.

'And I'd put my shitty paws into it before I realized what the hell it was,' the ex-Torgau man said bitterly.

'Must have been one of those rear-echelon stallions,' Schulze commented sympathetically. 'They crap all over the place.'

'Ner,' the ex-Torgau man answered. 'They never get that near the front – their hide's too precious.' He took a sip of his nigger's sweat. 'All I'm saying is that there ought to be the death penalty for that sort of thing! Who else but a first class crap hound with ingrowing toenails and flat feet would do that kind of thing – shitting indiscriminately for other fellers to fall into!'

'After the war when they start making the war films in Berlin, they ought to show the front like it really is,' one of the South Tyroleans said in his almost unintelligible mountain dialect. 'Parts of soldiers lying all around, people getting shot

* SS slang for the Russian multiple mortar (*transl.*).

while they're trying to take a shit – that kind of thing!'

'Yeah,' another young blond trooper supported him, 'and they should throw a little crap into the theatre's air-conditioning when they show it, so the civilians in the audience can smell what it was like on a battlefield too. Shitty!'

'Civvies don't want to know anything about us front line swine,' the ex-Torgau man said bitterly. 'They don't shitting well know and they don't shitting well care.'

Schulze lowered his fork, laden with fried potatoes.

'And I don't blame the poor bastards,' he said so softly that no one in the little group crouched around the heat glowing from the trench stove heard. 'It's better that no one knows what this kind of war is like.'

As the fifth day came and still the Amis had not attacked, Schulze and the ex-Torgau man, who had been sentenced to death in 1942 for striking an officer and had accepted recruitment into the Wotan as an alternative, organized the Battle Group's first beetle race. There were plenty of the repulsive, black, hard-shelled insects around. All the competitors needed to do was to dig a hole at the bottom of their foxholes and an hour later it would be alive with black wriggling beetles. The racing system was simple. The beetles' backs were painted different colours and then they were placed in a large jar. The jar itself was deposited in the centre of a large circle, raised and the first beetle out of the ring was judged to be the winner.

By the end of the first day of racing, Schulze had won over three hundred cigarettes, eight cans of 'Old Man', the standard issue meat ration, reputedly made of dead old men, and four pairs of sheer silk Italian black market stockings – 'and I'm going to draw them on myself, lads, every lovely centimetre of the wench's leg!' he had boasted, rolling his eyes lecherously.

But when the ex-docker had discovered that he was running out of the black syrup with which he had managed to dip the feet of the other men's beetles and thus slow them down, he had decided to withdraw from 'this season's racing', as he told the others, 'Regretfully.' Still the beetle racing craze caught on and it was during the afternoon 'Derby', the major race of the stand-down period, on the sixth day, the new officer appeared in their midst.

The race had just ended when a herd of black Italian pigs, chased up the rise by a puffing, red-faced Sergeant Metzger, the Battle Group's senior NCO, scuffled across the 'race course', crushing two of the 'favourites' under their hooves. There was an immediate outcry and Schulze cried:

'Where the hell did those cruddy pigs come from!' Then he pretended to catch sight of the big ex-butcher with the stupid wooden face for the first time and added in mock apology:

'Sorry, Sergeant Metzger, I didn't realize they were friends of yours!'

Metzger's red face turned crimson with rage, but he contained himself. The Hamburger knew too much about him from the days when they had been NCOs together before Schulze had decided to desert.

'Those cruddy pigs, Schulze, are Colonel Geier's – for your information. They cost this unit exactly one truckload of "Old Man" on the Macaroni black market. It had gone off, of course, but those stupid Italianos did not know that, did they?'

He grinned suddenly, his little piglike eyes full of peasant cunning.

'You're the smart one, Sergeant Metzger,' Schulze complimented him, winking surreptitiously at the grinning Tyrolean boys, who knew just how much he hated the Group's senior NCO. 'What would we all do without you, Sergeant! When do we get our piece of Schnitzel, then?' he added, licking his lips in mock anticipation. 'I'm getting sick of that Old Man and giddi-up soup*.'

'You don't, Schulze,' Metzger snapped flicking his stick across the rump of one of the black pigs, which was busily engaged in eating most of the entrants for the next race. 'These pigs are intended as our iron ration if we get cut off up here. It was Colonel Geier's idea.'

'So that you lads up at Twin Tits can fill yer guts on the sly, eh, Sergeant Metzger?'

* The usual midday soup in the Wehrmacht, supposedly made from horsemeat (*transl.*).

Metzger opened his mouth to bellow an angry retort, but another, softer voice beat him to it.

'That is a dangerous accusation – a very dangerous accusation to make, soldier,' it said. The Saxon accent was unmistakable.

Schulze and the rest swung round and stiffened to attention the next instant. The man who had spoken wore the stars of a second-lieutenant on his black collar patch, and the silver SS runes gleamed bright and new on his unwrinkled grey tunic, bare of any decorations save the War Service Cross, Third Class. For the first time since any of them had joined the Armed SS, they were facing an officer of that elite formation, who actually wore glasses.

'I didn't mean anything, sir,' Schulze said surprised, taking in the officer's pudgy face and the cunning eyes magnified by the thick lenses of the gold-rimmed spectacles.

'Everybody here knows that Sergeant Metzger was a butcher in civvie street. It's a bit of a standing joke among the men,' he ended lamely, disconcerted by the new officer's fixed unwinking stare.

Finally the second-lieutenant lowered his gaze. Taking a notebook and a silver pencil from his breast pocket, he asked:

'What's your name, soldier?'

'Schulze, Hans,' Schulze snapped, 'SS man!'

The officer made a note.

'I shall be keeping my eye on you, Schulze,' he said softly in his ugly Saxon accent. 'You'd better watch your step.'

'Yessir!'

And with that, he tugged at his mule's bridle and kicking one of the rooting black pigs out of his way with a polished boot, plodded up the slope towards the Twin Tits' CP.

'Who the hell's that when he's at home?' Schulze breathed when the strange officer was out of earshot.

The burly NCO grinned maliciously.

'That's our new National Socialist Leadership Officer, sent here from the Reich Main Security Office in Berlin. He's been sent to show you Bolshevik shits what it means to belong to the National Socialist elite.'

Schulze absorbed the information with a long face.

'And what is the National Socialist paragon's worthy name?' he asked.

'Second Lieutenant Kriecher.'

'Kriecher,' Schulze echoed the name thoughtfully. 'The name just fits the cunning little bastard.'

'Perhaps,' Metzger said and flicked his switch across the plump rump of the nearest pig. 'But you'd better watch your step, Schulze. He's got his eye on you, believe you me.'

Thus the 'Creeper'* entered the lives of the men of SS Assault Group Wotan. He was not sent out to one of the companies but was retained at Geier's CP, yet none of the rank-and-file seemed able to ascertain his true function, not even Sergeant Metzger. Most of his day he spent creeping around their positions, suddenly appearing behind a working party or in the midst of a stand-down group, head bent over his little black notebook, scribbling furiously with his silver pencil. The men grew to hate him, especially Schulze who took to spreading malicious jokes about him.

'Of course they'll take anybody in the SS these days,' he would crack to someone who had not heard the story before. 'Even little creeps like that. Why, didn't you hear the tale of the lad who went to see the medics with no arms and they still signed him up. And when he got to his unit, the adjutant said: "What, you've got no arms! Don't worry, there's a place for you in this battalion. Go over there and help those two soldiers pumping water in buckets." "But I can't help 'em, sir," the chap protested, "I've no arms." "Don't worry," the Adj answered. "Just tell 'em when to stop filling the buckets. You see they're both blind!" '

And he would follow up the joke with his own bitter assessment of Lieutenant Kriecher's motivation.

'Of course, you know the Creeper's trouble, don't yer? Too much five against one – the old right-handed widow!'

And when one of the Tyrolean mountain boys did not understand, he would explain with an explicit if obscene gesture.

'They all get like that in the end – too much looking through

* *Kriecher* is the German word for 'creeper' (*transl. note*).

keyholes and bashing away at it. That's the Creeper's problem, believe you me.'

Once Schulze attempted to tackle von Dodenburg on the true function of the mysterious officer, but the CO had shrugged and given him the same explanation as Metzger.

'National Socialist Leadership Officer, Schulze. Sent here personally by the Reichsführer SS to attempt to convert you heathen Bolsheviks to the true cause.'

'That'll be the day, sir!' Schulze had grunted. 'My old man in Barmbek would half slaughter me when I went home – *if* I ever do get home again off this sodding mountain.'

'Don't worry, Schulze,' von Dodenburg had laughed. 'You know the old saying? Weeds never die.'

'I wish that particular weed would!'

'Tut, tut,' von Dodenburg had commented without rancour, 'you should not say things like that about your superior officers.'

But in the end the big ex-docker's hatred of the little Saxon officer gave way to a kind of fear. Whenever the Creeper was near him, he could feel a cold finger of apprehension trace its way slowly down his spine and the hairs on the back of his head would stand up. He took to avoiding the man as much as possible, and he wasn't the only one.

The officers of the Wotan did not take to the newcomer, who always ate alone and did not join the rough horseplay of the little mess they had made for themselves in the big log-covered bunker behind the Twin Tits' command post. Whereas their conversation was devoted to women, drink and the technicalities of their calling, his was limited to harsh brittle comments which always began with, 'The Führer has stated that . . .' as if he alone had the ear of the Leader. Even Schwarz, the most fanatical of these young men who were the elite of National Socialist youth, could not get along with this strange officer who had appeared so suddenly in their midst.

But as the first week passed since their capture of Peak 555 and no Ami counter-attack from below had materialized, the young officers started to forget the Creeper and concentrate more on the unknown prospect that lay before them.

On the morning of the ninth day, with the clouds hanging

low over the peak, grey and leaden with snow, the Vulture sought out von Dodenburg in his own CP. Together they made a full inspection of their positions, their eyes straying continually to the smoke-filled valley below, trying to penetrate the secret of what lay behind the man-made screen.

'Very satisfactory,' the bandy-legged little cavalryman said when they came to the end of the perimeter and slapped his cane against his riding boots. 'The men have done a very good job, though I think we could do with one or two of our heavy mgs resiting.'

'I'll see to it immediately, sir,' von Dodenburg snapped.

'Good, better get it done before the violins start to play,' he indicated the rolling grey clouds with his cane.

For a while they walked in silence, broken only by the rumble of the heavies far off.

'What are we going to do about the Party, von Dodenburg?' the Vulture asked suddenly.

The younger officer turned startled.

'What did you say, sir?'

'I asked what are we going to do with the Party? You know, of course, that we're losing the war?' He said, as though he were discussing the state of the weather. 'If we're going to approach the Allies, then we've got to go to them with clean hands – relatively clean hands, that is. You understand?' He paused and taking out his monocle deliberately, began to rub off the condensation caused by the icy cold.

'No . . . no, I don't, sir.'

'It is simple. The Allies won't receive us with those men in Berlin still in power.'

'But that's a shocking suggestion, sir,' von Dodenburg burst out, his eyes filled with shocked outrage. 'You can't mean—'

'Of course I can, my dear young von Dodenburg,' Geier cut him short. 'The time has come when someone in authority has—' He broke off abruptly.

The pudgy figure of Lieutenant Kriecher had just appeared from behind one of the camouflaged heaps of ammunition boxes. Urgently, the Vulture clutched von Dodenburg's arm and forced him to commence walking again.

'Perhaps we should drop that subject for the time being, eh,' he said hastily. 'Our first task is to stop the Amis, then we can begin talking about – er – negotiations!'

Just as the Creeper caught up with them, notebook in hand as usual, he added quickly:

'We will let the mountain decide, von Dodenburg, when they come again – which they will undoubtedly do. Soon.'

SIX

The Americans came that same night. Like timber wolves through some great North American forest. Silently, hushing from shell-hole to shell-hole, the slight sounds they made in their rubber-soled boots, covered by the persistent hiss of the driving snow. Ex-cooks, carpenters, redcaps, bellhops, Southern sharecroppers, they fought their way up the steep slope against the snow which lashed their faces, determined to prove to the US Army that they were fighting men and not second-class citizens, only fit for rearline duties. For on this night the 93rd Infantry Regiment (Colored) was going into action for the first time.

'Black Jack' Jones, their skinny white CO at the point just behind the lead scout, could hardly see them now for the driving flakes. But he knew they were there behind him. He sensed them, and felt a warm glow of pride in his regiment, which had been laughed at, reviled, short-changed ever since he had formed it from the hordes of eager volunteers in Fort Jay. They were his men and not the boys, as the fat, contemptuous Alabaman full-bird on the Second Corps staff, who had given him his nickname of 'Black Jack', always called them. They were fighting men and no longer the cowed, segregated 'coons' he had taken over the year before.

Just ahead of him 'Pineapple Pete', the lead scout, a farm boy from Georgia, who had gained his nickname because his belt was heavy with fragmentation and phosphorous grenades, stopped abruptly and hissed:

'We've hit the wire, Colonel, sir!'

'*Freeze!*' Black Jack Jones ordered immediately.

Hastily Black Jack slung his carbine and crawled forward to where Pineapple Pete was crouched next to the snow-covered strands of wire, already fumbling with the wire-cutters.

'Okay, sir?'

'Okay, Pete.'

They dropped on to their backs in the white mess and took the strain together, each man gripping a handle of the big wire-cutters.

'Now, sir,' Pete grunted and exerted full pressure.

The first strand went with a loud snap. For an instant they waited, heads cocked to the wind listening, hearts thumping furiously. But there was no sound save that of the wind. The Krauts hadn't heard them.

'The next one,' Black Jack whispered.

Once again the black man and the white man lying in the snow on the barren Italian mountain side only fifty yards from the enemy positions, took the strain. It snapped easily and they crawled forward into the confused maze of wire, trailing toilet rolls behind them, as a guideline to the men who would follow.

Foot by foot they fought their way forward, the sweat streaming down their strained faces despite the bitter cold. Once Pineapple Pete knocked the cutters out of the Colonel's hand and whispered:

'Sorry, Colonel, sir, but them darned Krauts have got a can of pebbles fixed to that one – see!'

Black Jack strained his eyes and caught sight of the vague round shape, which indicated an enemy trap. If they had cut the wire, the can would have gone swinging back and forth – and presumably other similar cans hidden by the darkness too – warning the German sentries on the plateau above them.

'Good boy,' he hissed and caught himself too late. 'Good man, I mean, Pete! You must have eyes like hawk's.'

Carefully they snipped off the can and lowered it gently to the ground, then tackled the wire which supported it. They moved on and the first wave of the 93rd followed, with Black Jack praying his men weren't bunching too much. If the Krauts caught them now, it would be a massacre. But their luck held out. They were getting closer and closer to the summit, the driving snow still covering their approach and deadening any sound they made.

'Just one more to go, sir,' Pete chortled, 'and then I'm gonna give them nasty old German Krauts a taste of the sweetest pineapples ever to come out of Georgia.'

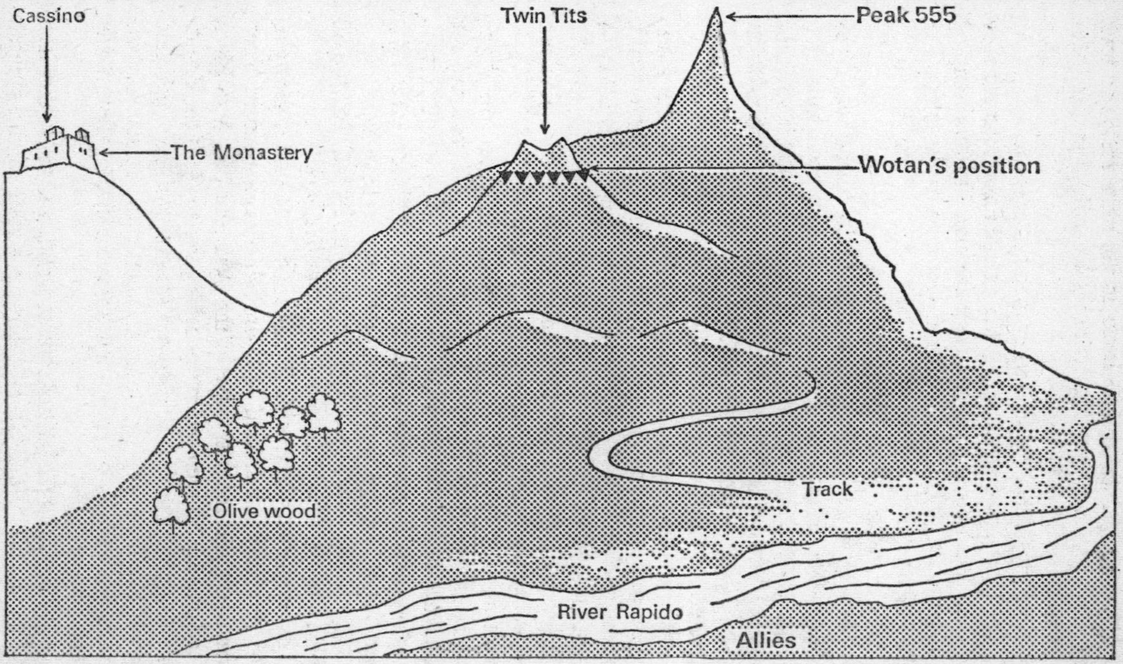
Cassino
Twin Tits
Peak 555
The Monastery
Wotan's position
Olive wood
Track
River Rapido
Allies

Black Jack grinned momentarily and took the strain once more.'

'Yeah,' he said, his voice strangely distorted. 'Just one more river to cross, Pete. Okay now!'

The wire gave with a snap. Next instant a sudden red light hushed into the sky, forcing apart the snow, bathing the men crouched in the wire blood-red.

'Christ!' Black Jack screamed in alarm and fear. 'Trip flare! Come on, fellers, follow me!'

He rose in panic, feverishly grabbing for his carbine. Pineapple Pete pulled out a grenade. But he never managed to throw it. The first high-pitched hysterical burst of enemy machine-gun fire caught him squarely in the belly. He screamed in agony. One of the phosphorous grenades on his belt exploded. A sheet of dazzling white flame rose up instantly and enveloped his body. In a second he was a writhing torch, illuminating the men frantically trying to fight their way through the wire, as the German perimeter erupted into violent life.

Schulze saw the Negro in the same instant as the Negro spotted him. He tore the pin out of the potato masher's base and flung it. His head hit the snow-covered ground in front of his pit and he counted frantically.

'Twenty ... twenty-one ... twenty-two ... twenty-three—'

The grenade exploded with a vivid flash just in front of him. Redhot, razor-sharp splinters of steel hissed through the air. His head felt as if it must burst the confines of his helmet. The blast hit him in the face like a wet fist. Automatically he opened his mouth to prevent his eardrums from bursting. In that same instant the Negro was tossed high into the night. When he came down again, he was minus both arms. But there were more behind him.

Schulze grabbed for his spandau, suddenly blinded by the flash of the exploding grenade. It wasn't there! The explosion had blown it away from its stand. Suddenly panic-stricken as the grunts and shouts in the strange language grew closer, he fumbled for his bayonet.

'There's one of the bastards over here!' a voice shouted only ten metres or so away.

He understood nothing but 'here'. The Amis had spotted him! Vaulting out of the pit, he drew his bayonet, legs spread apart, and waited.

Two of them suddenly burst through the cloud of snow. The leading man lunged immediately with his rifle. Schulze felt a sharp stab of pain along his thigh. Something wet and hot gushed down his leg. Yelping with pain, he raised his big nailed 'dice beaker'* and kicked the Ami between the legs. He screamed in agony and shot backwards into the snow, rolling himself in a ball, twisting and turning and clutching his testicles. Schulze sprang over him and parried the other man's thrust. But the Ami was quick on his toes. He dodged to one side and swinging his rifle round, thrust at Schulze with the brass-shod butt.

Schulze turned his head just in time. The M-I caught him a glancing blow on the shoulder. Another man would have gone reeling back. Not Schulze. He knew that he was done for, once he fell to the ground. Instead, he lunged forward. His bayonet connected with something hard. The Negro howled with pain. His rifle fell from his nerveless fingers. Schulze had severed the tendons of his right wrist.

In that same instant, however, the Negro thrust his boot into Schulze's belly, as if he were a male dancer doing a high kick, and grabbing the German's tunic pulled him down on top of himself. Schulze's nostrils were assailed by a heavy pungent odour, compounded of sweat and some kind of perfume. The Negro was fumbling in his pocket with his free hand. Schulze could guess what he was after. He tried to grab the hand, and missed. Something gleamed in the thin white light. A cut-throat razor! Schulze felt the hair at the back of his head stand up in fear. His big left hand shot out and grabbed the Negro's wrist. His other, the first two fingers extended stiffly like the prongs of a fork, thrust up and into the man's nostrils. They found their target. Schulze ripped the wet cavities upwards.

The Negro's scream of agony was drowned in the sudden stream of blood which threatened to choke him. The cut-throat

* German Army slang for the jackboot (*transl.*).

razor dropped into the snow, as he writhed with pain. Schulze did not give him a second chance. He grabbed the razor, and pulling harder at the man's nostrils so that his contorted face was drawn back to expose the throat, he slashed the razor across it just above the adam's apple. Once – twice – three times, while the Negro's legs writhed helplessly.

Seconds later the Ami's body went limp. He was dead. Schulze pulled his fingers from the Negro's nose and let himself fall into the snow beside his victim. Too exhausted to fight any more, hating the dead man so bitterly for having made him do this terrible thing.

The attack on the German perimeter had developed into a bloody, bitter series of hand-to-hand fights between individual soldiers, swaying back and forth locked in desperate battle in front of the foxhole line, wreathed in the howling white fury of the snow. Neither side gave or expected quarter. When a soldier went down, his opponent rained blow after blow on his unprotected face until it turned a horrifying pulp. Rifles were abandoned for anything – bayonet, knife, entrenching tool – with which they could gouge, slash, chop, hack, slice. A frenzied blood-lust overcame the terrified men, German and American, fighting up on the naked mountain top, transforming them into wild animals from whose throats came frantic, unintelligible grunts.

In his CP, all communication lost with the perimeter, a shaken von Dodenburg tried to restore contact with his outposts. In the yellow flickering light the sweating, trembling operator tried to raise them over and over again while von Dodenburg paced up and down puffing nervously at a cigar.

'Hello three . . . hello three . . . do you hear my signal? . . . Hello four . . . hello four, do you hear my signal . . .?'

But neither three nor four – nor any of the other outposts which had a radio link with the CP answered.

'Listen,' von Dodenburg snapped, grabbing at the operator's shoulder so that he would pay attention.

The young soldier pulled off one earphone. Von Dodenburg could see his eyes were round and staring with fear.

'Get Colonel Geier on the radio. Tell him we've lost contact with the companies. Tell him too that I'm going up to have a look myself. Request that he stand by with reinforcements, if necessary, as the situation is highly confused. Get that, operator?'

Von Dodenburg swung round, putting on his helmet and grabbing his machine-pistol at the same time, and snapped to Lieutenant Kriecher who was squatting on a ration box in the dim corner of the CP.

'Kriecher, I want you to come with me. If I get hit, you'll have to take over.'

The National Socialist Leadership Officer looked at him, as if he had gone crazy.

'Come on, man. Heaven, arse and twine, hurry it up!' von Dodenburg roared and flung him the other Schmeisser lying on the trestle table.

The Creeper made no attempt to catch it. It clattered to the floor. Behind him the operator started to rap out his call sign.

'Hello, Snowdrop, can you hear me Snowdrop? . . . This is Sunray calling. I repeat, can you hear me Snowdrop . . .?'

Von Dodenburg looked down at the other officer, shocked and not a little puzzled.

'What's the matter with you, Kriecher?' he rapped. 'Come on, man, for Christ's sake, speak up!'

The Creeper's eyes were wild with fear behind the thick lenses of his gold-rimmed glasses.

'Come on, Lieutenant Kriecher,' von Dodenburg thundered, beside himself with rage. 'Get the lead out of your fat arse!'

'But you can't make me . . . me fight,' the Creeper found his voice at last. 'I'm not a fighting soldier.'

'Well in Heaven's name, what the hell are you then?'

Von Dodenburg never got an answer to his question.

'Look out sir,' the operator screamed suddenly. '*A grenade!*'

A round metallic ball had tumbled to the ground just inside the entrance to the command post. Von Dodenburg reacted instinctively, his body electric with fear. Grabbing the helmet off the table, he flung himself forward, thrust it over the grenade and pressed down hard with all his weight.

A second later the grenade exploded. With a kick like that of a mule, the impact struck him in the chest. His whole body was lifted up from the ground. The air was full of the smell of burning. As he came down again and the shattered helmet rolled from beneath him, he saw what it was – the camouflage paint, melted by the hot blast.

'Are you all right, sir,' the operator yelled, pulling him to his feet.

Von Dodenburg swayed groggily and looked down at his chest. The whole front of his tunic was black and singed.

'I think so,' he said weakly.

Then he shook his ringing head. There wasn't a moment to lose. The Amis would come bursting in in a moment, spraying the CP with machine-pistol fire.

'Give me the Schmeisser,' he ordered, his voice sounding faint and far away. 'And stand by!'

In the very same instant that the man who had thrown the grenade pulled back the tarpaulin, von Dodenburg fired a wild burst from the hip. The clatter of the slugs was ear-splitting in the confined space. The big Ami screamed with agony and came tumbling down the crude steps to sprawl dead in front of von Dodenburg. Hastily he kicked him over to make sure. He was. The bottom half of his face had been shot away.

'Come on,' he yelled, recovering himself now, 'let's get the hell out of here. It's sheer suicide to stay!'

Now even the Creeper needed no urging. He grabbed the machine-pistol from the floor and followed the other two up the stairs.

Outside the snow storm still raged. Here and there, little groups of shadowily outlined men swayed back and forth in mortal combat but the Amis were already pulling back. Everywhere their officers were blowing shrill blasts on their whistles and shouting orders. A Negro sat up suddenly just in front of them, moaning piteously, his arm shot away, blood pouring through fingers clasped to the stump. Von Dodenburg shot him without even realizing he was doing so.

They pushed on. Before them in the white mist, he could hear the confused orders and counter-orders of the retreating Amis. They were definitely withdrawing. Hastily he pulled out his signal pistol and fired a red marker flare into the sky.

'Rally on me, Wotan!' he bellowed above the vicious snap-and-crackle of small-arms fire. *'On me, Wotan – now!'*

Grenadiers came scurrying out of the snow on all sides, firing wildly from the hip as they came.

'Form a skirmish line,' he yelled, 'and stop that bloody indiscriminate firing, will you!'

The firing petered away as the men took up their positions.

'I'll take the right, Kriecher – you the left!'

This time the officer did not protest. He took his position up as ordered and when von Dodenburg blew a shrill blast to advance, he ran forward obediently with the rest.

Here and there small groups of the Americans fought to the end. But the men of Wotan knew they were winning now; they had the Amis on the run. They charged forward, ignoring the slugs which hissed by them. Men crumpled violently, but in their rage they did not seem to notice their casualties. A big black sergeant, face streaked with blood, tried to cover the withdrawal with a Thompson sub-machine-gun. A bareheaded blond trooper swung a shovel at him and sliced his face almost in half with the keen blade.

A couple of Negroes almost hidden in captured foxholes held them up for a few minutes with well-directed fire from their BAR. But an SS man pulled the china ring from a stick grenade, counted four aloud and flung it hissing in their direction. The two disappeared in a blinding burst of flame. When it cleared the two Amis lay there, mangled and bleeding. Someone finished them off with a vicious high-pitched burst from a Schmeisser.

And then, suddenly, the Negroes broke completely. Streaming wildly down the snowy mountain side, skidding and sliding, they threw away their weapons, fighting each other to get away from that terrible fire, carrying their officers and NCOs with them; and behind them the Nationalist Socialist Leadership officer began to go from one wounded Negro to the next, turning their heads gently, pressing his pistol against their cropped heads just behind the right ear and blowing out their brains.

The American artillery reacted at once. With a roar like that of an infuriated beast cheated of its prey, the guns of the Second Corps opened up.

The veterans of the Wotan Battle Group knew that strange sound well enough. Paralysis descended upon their positions at once. The rattle of their spandaus died immediately. The crews huddled together expectantly, their heads buried in the stinking uniformed body of the man next to them. In the rifle pits, the troopers cowered in the mud, bodies rolled into tense balls, trying to present the smallest possible target. In that same instant, the first hundred or so heavy shells straddled the perimeter, bursting in a deafening thunder. Immediately all hell was let loose. Purple searing flame, the choking smell of cordite, pieces of shrapnel and copper shellbands hissing through the air, as big as a man's fist, slashing showers of earth and mud. Mangled, screaming men were flung high into the air.

A platoon of rear echelon stallions approaching the Twin Tits' HQ, carrying the breakfast rations for the Vulture's staff, were caught by a direct hit. Black army ration loaves and the kettles of hot giddiup soup flying crazily through the vicious storm. A runner was caught out in the open, his head severed neatly by a piece of glowing metal. A group of reinforcements, boots polished, rifles neatly oiled, running panic-stricken through the hellish barrage and taking casualties all the way, dropped gasping into the perimeter trenches, dirty, bloodied and already completely demoralized.

In the Twin Tits' CP the assembled officers looked at each other, faces pale with shock, eyes wide and staring, as the big dugout shook and swayed with each explosion like a ship at sea hitting wave after wave. In the corner, the Creeper crouched in the foetal position, knees tucked up tightly under his chin, eyes closed, and hands pressed tightly to his lips. Next to him, Metzger, his normally ruddy face now drawn and ashen-grey, took surreptitious gulps from his bottle of *grappa*, his one consolation in this crazy murderous front-line world.

But despite the tremendous barrage, the Vulture was his usual self. Calmly he polished his monocle, and seizing a brief pause in the shelling, rasped:

'You have done well gentlemen. I am pleased with you. Our defences have held well.'

'But they were only niggers – little better than Jews and animals,' Schwarz said contemptuously. 'There is no victory in defeating such creatures.'

The Vulture looked across at the one-armed captain almost sadly. Everyone in the Battle Group knew now that Schwarz was mad; he had to be treated gently.

'No you are wrong, Captain,' he said. 'The black men were very brave, but poorly led and inexperienced. After all they did penetrate our positions.'

He turned to the others.

'One thing we have learned this night, however, is that we need more strength. If we had had the new paratroop recoilless rifle, we could have broken up the Ami attack much more easily. We need more beef. But that problem will be taken care of later. As soon as this barrage lifts, I want you to get back to your men immediately.'

'You mean they'll come back, sir?' von Dodenburg asked.

'Of course,' the Vulture said easily and slapped his cane against the side of his riding boot. 'Believe you me, gentlemen, we haven't seen the last of our black friends from the land of the boundless possibilities this night . . .'

'Hello, Sunray . . . This is Moonbeam . . . Hello, Sunray, this is Moonbeam, are you receiving me?'

The radio operator, crouched in the cover of the snowbank at the bottom of the mountain called over and over again, while the officers of the 93rd came and went, reporting the terrible losses the Regiment had suffered.

'First company, Second Battalion – twenty killed, fifty wounded, thirty missing . . . First Battalion, sir, three officers and six noncoms unwounded . . .'

Black Jack Jones slumped behind the operator, the blood pouring down from the gash on his forehead, received the news of the terrible casualties blankly, as if they had happened to someone else's regiment and not to his own beloved 93rd. In the shelter of a poncho, the regimental surgeon was sawing off the leg of an eighteen-year-old runner. He could hear the harsh grate of the bone-saw on the boy's leg bone and his rapid, shallow breathing.

'Hello Moonbeam,' a voice broke through the static suddenly. 'Hello Moonbeam . . . Here Sunray.'

Black Jack Jones shook himself out of his lethargy. He grabbed the mike from the operator's frozen hand.

'Hello Sunray, here Moonbeam. Are you receiving me?'

'Sure, I'm receiving you,' a well-remembered, satisfied Southern voice answered. 'Your boys sure did get their black asses whupped, colonel, didn't they!' The staff colonel's voice, distorted as it was by the static, was unmistakably gleeful. 'I told you they would. Yer can't make fighting men out of that kind of material.'

Black Jack Jones exploded with rage.

'Get off the radio, damn you!' he cried, forgetting radio procedure completely. 'I want to speak to the Corps Commander!'

'Who the hell do you think you're talking to, Colonel!' the fat staff officer cried.

'I know who I'm talking to – a mean bastard of a bigot whom I'm personally gonna pistol-whip when I come to Corps HQ. Now get your ass off this radio – quick!'

The staff colonel blustered but he fetched Keyes to the radio. Underneath the poncho the surgeon had finished with the boy. A blood-stained orderly deposited the severed limb in the snow, and as the boy was carried out, another soldier with most of his lower jaw shot away, was led in.

'Listen, General,' Black Jack snapped, 'I need all the artillery support you can give in thirty minutes. I want that goddam peak slapped with everything you've got.'

'You're going in again, Moonbeam?'

'Yes,' Black Jack said.

'What are your casualties like?'

'Bad, hellishly bad, sir. My First Battalion has had it. The Second is still capable of combat. The Third is in good shape. I'm jumping off with the Third.'

Black Jack could almost hear Keyes thinking.

'You were at the Point, weren't you, Jones? You're a regular?'

'Yessir.'

'Don't you know that you're in a bad enough hole now as it is. The 93rd is a publicity exercise in the final analysis. If you can get them out without any more casualties, you'll save your career. But if you go in again and get plastered again, you've had it.'

Keyes' harsh, monotonous voice became gentler. The old cavalryman had a soft spot in his heart for determined young officers, especially if they were from West Point as he was and three generations of Keyes before him.

'It'd be kinda foolish to ruin your career, Jack, for a bunch of – well, you know what I mean?'

'I appreciate your concern, sir. But my 93rd is going to take that damned peak or—' Jones hesitated a moment – 'or I shan't be coming back, sir.'

'All right, Colonel, be it on your own head. I'll give you all the support I can. I'll call TAC Air Force, but I don't think we'll get much change there for aerial support. This weather's too lousy. But you can rely on the corps artillery. When are you going in, Colonel?'

'Dawn, sir.'

'Dawn, eh? OK. It's on your head – and the best of luck, Jack . . .'

'Ah don't see why the folks back in the States always rave about this country,' the skinny PFC from Georgia snorted. 'Jesus Christ on the mountain, there ain't nothing here we don't have better back home!'

'Yeah, in a pig's eye!' his buddy, a smart high yellow from Chicago snapped from the side of his mouth. 'Go and tell that one to the marines, Washington, they might believe ya.' He lapsed into silence to keep pace with the long line of khaki-clad men climbing up the snow-covered mountain.

Black Jack Jones, his head bandaged now looked over his shoulder. Is this all that's left of the Regiment, he asked himself in dull surprise, seeing the extent of his losses for the first time. He glanced to his right. The Second was keeping up despite the rough going and the artillery which was coming in low over their heads. They surmounted an embankment and the last shells from the Corps' barrage started to hide the smoke-obscured peak. A machine-gun up ahead chattered suddenly. Here and there soldiers began to flop down behind the cover.

'Off your duffs!' the big Staff Sergeant, who had insisted he should carry the regimental flag into action, snarled. 'The mother-fugging war ain't over yet. *Move it!*'

Some of the young soldiers bent their heads to the glittering snow and pretended that he wasn't there. The Staff Sergeant smashed his boot into the high yellow PFC's side. 'On your-doggon feet, soldier!' he snapped, 'you goddam nigger, you!'

The line moved forward again, more hurriedly now. The chatter of the machine-guns increased in intensity. The icy clear morning air was full of lead. Men began to fall everywhere.

The Third hesitated for a moment, the men staring in apparent bewilderment at the men lying on the snow, their blood staining it red, as if they could not understand how this terrible thing could happen to them.

'Come on, follow me,' Black Jack Jones yelled. 'Keep moving, men!'

But half the Battalion was down in the snow now, firing at the smoke-shrouded peak. The ones who had kept advancing, faltered and they too were running back to their comrades, sobbing for breath, crashing into the snow beside the others and firing their weapons furiously as if this were sufficient excuse for their withdrawal.

'Oh, you yella-bellied bunch of niggers!' the Staff Sergeant with the regimental flag cursed. 'Why, yer nothing more than a—' He never finished the sentence. He swayed crazily suddenly, as a bullet struck him in the back. Blood spurted out of his mouth and he fell forward onto the snow. 'You niggers,' he said faintly, then died.

The high yellow from Chicago grabbed the flag, now stained with the dead man's blood. He scrambled warily to his feet and looked numbly at Black Jack.

The Colonel did not seem to see the bullets striking the snow in spurts all around him as he walked along the long line of men lying down, as if he were back on parade in Fort Jay.

'Come on men,' he kept saying, raising his calm voice only when the chatter of the machine-guns threatened to drown it. 'Only another hundred yards and we've got them. For the sake of the old ninety-third.'

A bullet struck his wrist and he dropped his carbine in the snow. He did not seem to notice, but kept on walking.

'All you've got to do is to get to your feet and start walking – walking after me. I'll lead you.'

'For the sake of the old Ninety-Third,' the high yellow soldier yelled and swung the flag.

'*For the Ninety-Third!*' they bellowed as one, scrambling to their feet.

'Follow me!' Black Jack Jones cried joyfully, waving his good arm towards the enemy.

The survivors of the 93rd swept forward and, as the smoke cleared in front of them, they caught sight of their enemy for the first time, white camouflaged helmets and thin dark perforated Machine-gun barrels which quivered with heat and scorched the snow. Then they charged into the pitiless fire.

But they were no match for the veterans of the Wotan, whose vicious hail of fire poured into their ever thinning ranks, cutting them down into small scattered groups, then into individuals, each man suddenly alone in the confused noise and smoke, doubling blindly forward to his death.

The boy from Georgia was stopped at a low stone wall. His friend, the high yellow with the flag, was mown down a second later. Someone else grabbed it. He stumbled forward with the few who were left, his face upturned to the peak in agony, hands clawing at the wall. He was shot just as he had managed to swing his leg over it. As he fell, a helmetless Black Jack seized it, without even a glance at him or the rest of the dead littering the wall all around him.

'Forward the old Ninety-Third,' he croaked crazily. '*Forward!*'

A bullet struck him in the shoulder. He staggered but kept on advancing. The ones who were still on their feet now followed. They scaled the wall and plunged through the snow after him, stumbling towards the machine-guns, as if they were eager to die.

Only a half a dozen of them reached the perimeter; and within a matter of minutes they were all dead, their Colonel in their midst, his bloody hands still gripping the flag. Behind, the regiment he had trained so lovingly lay sprawled dead or dying on the snow-covered slope of Peak 555 stark against its white surface, while the handful of wounded survivors hobbled painfully and silently like sleep walkers down the way they had come. The 93rd Infantry Regiment (Colored) existed no more.

Four hours later, von Dodenburg, accompanied by Schulze as a bodyguard against the Italian partisans who were beginning to make a nuisance of themselves on Route Nine, was heading north in the Battle Group's Volkswagen jeep. His orders from the Vulture were simple – in part. He was to take the captured banner and present it to the Reichsführer SS personally.

'Herr Himmler likes such trappings of military grandeur,' the Vulture had remarked cynically. 'Perhaps he will hang it with the rest of the mumbo-jumbo in that crypt he has built himself in the Wewelsburg*, what?'

In return he was to ask the Reichsführer SS for an immediate delivery of the recoilless rifles which were still on the secret list, but which, Geier knew, were being delivered to all airborne units, including the SS Parachute Battalion.

But that had not been the Vulture's only order. As they had walked across the plateau towards the mules, which were to take him and Schulze down to the valley and the Battle Group's rear echelon, he had gripped von Dodenburg's arm just short of the place where the sweating SS troopers were throwing the Americans' stiffening bodies into a communal grave.

'Von Dodenburg, a word in your ear.'

He had indicated with a nod that the Creeper should move away and had waited till he was out of earshot. Then he had whispered:

'Von Dodenburg, I know that you believe in the National Socialist cause implicitly, but you are also a simple soldier like

* A castle in Westphalia, housing the tombs of several Saxon kings, which Himmler had restored because he believed he was descended from one of them.

myself, one who believes in Germany's destiny. Am I right, my friend?'

The young Major had mumbled something and waited, bewildered by the sudden mystery, for what was to come.

'When you have seen that fool of a Reichsführer, I want you to see Group Leader Schellenberg.'

'The head of the SD?'

'Yes.'

'And what shall I say, sir?'

'Nothing. Just tell him you come from the – er – Vulture,' he grinned faintly. 'He, knowing Schellenberg, will do the talking, believe me.'

Thus mystified, von Dodenburg swept north towards Rome's airport where they would catch the military courier plane for Berlin and Himmler's HQ. But if von Dodenburg was glum and silent, Schulze, Schmeisser cradled ready for the Italian partisans should they have the audacity to attack an SS vehicle, was jubilant. More than once he exploded joyfully:

'Great crap on the Christmas tree, sir, we're going home – home to mother!'

Two: The Traitors

'Of course, it's treason, Kuno . . . But it must be done for the sake of our country. '*General von Dodenburg to his son Major von Dodenburg.*

ONE

Berlin was dying. As the ancient wood-burning cab, with its steaming boiler trundling after it on a trailer, left Tempelhof Air Field, von Dodenburg and Schulze could see that the nation's capital lay in ruins.

'Oh my aching arse,' Schulze breathed. 'It's worse than Hamburg! Those RAF Tommies have really knocked the shit out of the place.'

Von Dodenburg nodded grimly and stared out at the sallow-faced undernourished men and women, their heads ducked in the collars of their shabby coats, who were hurrying through the ruins which still smouldered here and there from the last air raid.

They did not look like the well-fed, exuberant Berliners, who had welcomed them back from France in 1940, screaming their hoarse, frantic *Sieg Heils*, as the survivors of the Wotan had goose-stepped down the *Unter den Linden.*

'They don't look so good, sir,' Schulze said dolefully. 'None too good at all.'

'No, they don't,' he agreed, watching an old woman in a rusty-black coat, wearily shovelling up the 'apple' left by a tired, lean-ribbed nag pulling a *Wehrmacht* transport. 'They're bearing a heavy burden. God knows how they do it, Schulze.'

Happy at the thought he would be soon home in Hamburg on a surprise forty-eight hour leave, Schulze chortled:

'Well, they always say that the bombs are worse, sir. Why, at the front, everything's in butter – a rest cure.'

'Get on with you,' von Dodenburg said with a tired smile, as the ancient wood-burning taxi started to draw up in front of the shattered *Lehrter Bahnhof*, where Schulze would catch his train for Hamburg.

They shook hands under the suspicious eyes of the two chain-dogs, guarding the entrance on the look-out for the deserters swarming through the capital. It wasn't every day that they saw an SS Major shake hands with a private soldier, but then it wasn't every day that they saw a private with the precious black and white Knight's Cross hanging round his neck.

'All right, Schulze, don't forget that you've only got forty-eight hours. I expect you back here – on this spot – at sixteen hundred hours exactly, two days from now. And don't bring back any souvenirs from those – er – *ladies* of yours in St Pauli.* Clear?'

'Clear as thick ink, sir,' Schulze said cheekily, slinging his rucksack, laden with Italian black market goods, over his big shoulder. 'I'll probably spend my leave in the station mission, caring for fallen angels.' He winked. 'My regards to the Reichsführer.'

Major von Dodenburg got back into the cab and snapped at the elderly driver:

'All right, Number Ten Prinz Albercht Strasse.'

The driver gave him a quick look, a sudden light of fear in his tired eyes. He knew the address well enough. It was the home of the Third Reich's police apparatus, the headquarters of the Gestapo itself.

'Well, man, what are you waiting for?' von Dodenburg snapped, angry at the naked look of fear on the man's worn face. What had he to be afraid of? The Gestapo was there only to protect the law-abiding folk comrades, not to hound them, as many stupid people thought.

* The Hamburg red-light district (*transl.*).

'Just thinking where it is, sir,' the driver said hastily and slid behind the seat.

But he did not even have time to wait for a tip after the cab had pulled up in front of the four-storey building, which had once housed an art academy, and was now the home of the Reich Main Security Office.

Himmler, the Reichsführer SS, saw him almost at once. As usual the ex-chicken farmer who was now the most feared man in Europe was correct and exceedingly well informed. He accepted the flag, as if he had known all along that it was on its way, gave von Dodenburg a brief lecture on the inferiority of the Negro race, full of the anthropological jargon he had picked up in these last years, and then asked:

'Well, my dear Major, what do you want for this?' He gave von Dodenburg a wintery smile, but his dark eyes did not light up behind the thick lenses of his pince-nez. 'I am sure that Colonel Geier would not dispense with such a useful officer as yourself to bring me a flag, eh?'

The tall adjutants in their trim black uniforms, grouped behind the Reichsführer, allowed themselves a polite titter; it wasn't often that Himmler made an attempt at a joke. When he did, they knew he expected a reaction; and they obviously had no intention of being sent to the Russian front by a suddenly enraged Reichsführer.

'No sir,' von Dodenburg said. 'Colonel Geier has a request to make through me.'

'And it is?'

'The new recoilless rifle. The Colonel believes that the SS Parachute Battalion is being equipped with it. He would like as many as possible for Wotan. They would be ideal for the kind of terrain we are defending in Italy.'

Himmler frowned and looked down at the detailed list of the gold watches, teeth, wedding rings, etc., which had been 'collected' from the National Socialist concentration camps stretching now all over occupied Europe.

'He would, would he? And why should the Parachute Battalion sacrifice its weapons to the Wotan, may I ask?'

Von Dodenburg flushed, as the adjutants smiled at his discomfort. He wished suddenly he could get a few of them back with him in the battalion; he would show them what the war was really like. Especially the young captain to the left of Himmler's chair, who was a magnificent physical specimen, just short of two metres in height.

'Because, Reichsführer, our need is greater than that of the Para Battalion. Our position is the key to the whole Cassino front. If Peak 555 is taken, then Cassino must fall – and, Reichsführer, I don't need to tell you what that would mean,' he added grimly.

'I take your point, Major,' Himmler said thoughtfully. 'I can understand your concern too, but my dear young man, you must not exaggerate the situation in Italy. In the Middle Ages, Germany's future was decided there once before because of our weakness and the damnable influence of the Catholic Church. But since then the time has changed. We have that damned black Pope and his Curia in our hands like that. And we are no longer weak. No, von Dodenburg, even when we are faced with half the world in coalition against us. Think back to the days of the Old Fritz*.'

Von Dodenburg sighed and let the lecture descend upon him, full of historical allusions to previous centuries which had little or nothing to do with Germany's present perilous situation; but in the end, when von Dodenburg thought the Reichsführer would never stop, the Head of the SS broke off in mid-sentence and snapped:

'You shall have the weapons, Major. Wagner,' he turned to the big captain, 'take care of the matter with the Major, will you.'

'Reichsführer!' barked the captain at the top of his voice, as if he were back on the parade ground at Bad Toelz and not in the tight confines of Himmler's office.

Himmler picked up his fountain pen again.

'Ensure, Major von Dodenburg, that the recoilless rifles are used to the best advantage. We must prevent the barbarians ever reaching the sacred soil of the Reich. Mark that!'

'I will, Reichsführer,' von Dodenburg barked, hardly able

* The reference is to Frederick the Great, the great Prussian king of the eighteenth century, who was Himmler's idol (*transl.*).

to believe that he had pulled it off after all. 'Thank you, Reichsführer. Heil Hitler!'

A few moments later he was out in the dark corridor again, dwarfed by the bulk of the black-clad adjutant striding in silence towards the door. The guards clicked to attention and von Dodenburg handed his special pass back to the NCO in charge. It was only then that his escort spoke.

'Silly old bastard, isn't he?' he said in a warm cultivated voice quite unlike the paradeground bellow he had just used in Himmler's office. 'Sometimes I feel like going up the wall when he runs off at the mouth like that about history. And in reality, he doesn't know his chicken farmer's arse from his knobbly elbow.'

Von Dodenburg stopped and looked up at him in bewilderment.

'What did you say, Captain?'

Wagner steered him on gently but firmly.

'It isn't wise to stand and talk in this building, Major,' he said. 'The front is a great deal safer than Number Ten Prinz Albrecht Strasse for those who disagree with our beloved Reichsführer SS. Believe you me, though,' he grinned impudently, 'I have so far had the good fortune not to be sent to that place, which they tell me is exceeedingly uncouth.'

'Exceedingly,' von Dodenburg said, flinging off the captain's hand. 'Now then, Wagner, what in devil's name is this all about?'

Wagner glanced hastily up and down the long corridor, dark where the windows were boarded up as a result of the RAF bombing raids. The cynical smile was still on his lips, but there was no hiding the anxious look in his eyes.

'The Vulture sent you here, Major, not only to collect a few artillery pieces, but also some information which is far more explosive than all the recoilless rifles in the Para Battalion's armoury.'

'And what is that supposed to mean?' von Dodenburg snapped, growing angry. 'Can't you speak plain German, man?'

'If I did, Major, my rather precious and somewhat handsome head would no longer be on these shoulders.' He raised his hand pleadingly. '*Pace*, all will be explained in due course. Please have patience. Group Leader Schellenberg will brief you.'

'And where will I find the Group Leader?'

Wagner dipped a hand in his pocket and pulled out a card. 'Here.'

Von Dodenburg stared down at the visiting card with the two words 'Salon Kitty' engraved upon it in a rather florid style.

"Salon Kitty, what the devil's that?'

Wagner grinned.

'Salon Kitty,' he said casually, 'oh, that's our own private brothel, Major.'

TWO

Forage cap at the back of his neck, tunic ripped open, rucksack slung carelessly, his breath reeking of *Korn*, Schulze barged into the first queue of eager servicemen lining up for the whores' services.

'No naked lights within fifteen metres,' he bellowed joyously, 'or we all go up in flames!'

'Sodding SS,' a burly undersized Obermaat in the submarine service growled in a thick waterfront accent, 'take yer shitty turn like the rest of us. We've all got dirty water on our chests, you know, you SS hero!'

Schulze placed a big hand in the sailor's face and shoved. The Obermaat went staggering backwards and sat down suddenly in the Herbertstrasse's dirty overflowing gutter.

'I know, milord*. But I wouldn't like to stick mine where you've had your dirty naval periscope.'

The garishly attired whores leaning out of the windows of the street of brothels, not far from Hamburg's Dammtor station where Schulze had descended in hurry five minutes before, laughed hysterically. Schulze threw off his cap with an expansive gesture and bowed.

'You'll be laughing on the other side of your faces, ladies, when you see what I've brought home for you from the front.' Drunkenly he yelled the traditional Hamburg greeting, '*Hummel, Hummel!*'

'*Mors, Mors* – arse, arse!' they screamed in delight.

Schulze turned to the handful of middle-aged Wehrmacht men standing in front of him.

'All right, you rear stallions, what about giving a front-line swine a break?' he chortled, doubling his fist significantly. 'I've limped here all the way from Dammtor. My need is great. You understand?' He spat on his knuckles slowly.

The Wehrmacht men got out of his way hurriedly.

* German Army slang term for a sailor (*transl.*).

'Of course, of course – we understand.'

'I knew you would,' Schulze grinned and slung his rucksack more firmly over his shoulder.

Inside, the house was obviously doing booming business. Fat middle-aged maids were running back and forth, carrying bottles and cigarettes. Whores in various stages of undress were moving up and down the dingy stairs, escorting eager or tired soldiers. Somewhere rusty bed springs were squeaking frantically.

'What's going on,' Schulze cried to the middle-aged Madam in the black silk with her dyed frizzed hair. 'On overtime or something? Or does the Führer need more cannon fodder?'

'Aren't you gonna take off yer pack?' the Madam asked sourly. 'You men haven't even got time to take yer boots off!'

'It's total war, mother. Everyone has got to make sacrifices, you know. I'll take my pack off afterwards. Now then, where's the girls?'

The Madam cupped her beringed fat hands round her mouth and shouted above the noise:

'Gerda, customers!' She turned to Schulze. 'That'll be ten marks and a mark for the Parisian*.'

'Only one!' Schulz exclaimed, as the girl emerged from the gloom, clad in a bra and red panties with black lacing. 'Here,' he pulled out a can of Italian coffee, 'give me the whole shitty packet! With the flanks that mare has got on her, I'll need half a dozen just to get her warmed up, won't I, my little cheetah!' he added, putting his big arm around the girl's ample breasts.

The Madam opened her mouth to protest, but when she saw the coffee, she hesitated.

'Real bean coffee?'

'Real bean coffee,' Schulze said airily, his fingers already fumbling with Gerda's left nipple. 'Picked every one myself.'

'All right.' The Madam shoved him the whole packet of *Vulkan* across the counter. 'But remember you pay extra for each additional jump!'

'And I thought this was the Red Cross! Come on, Gerda, show me the way to paradise, will you, and let me get through

* Parisian: Army slang for a contraceptive (*transl.*).

them pearly gates. I've been saving this up for over two months now and my tonsils are beginning to float.'

He followed her up the gloomy rickety stairs, admiring her long legs, clad in black silk stockings and told himself once again that women were excitement enough; why did men need war?

'Business is good, eh?' he asked.

'Always will be as long as you men want to have your dirty way with us women.'

They reached her room and the whore kicked the door closed with the heel of her shoe. Slipping off her red panties, she flopped on the brass bed which sagged wearily under her weight. In a routine voice, her eyes fixed on the flaking ceiling, her legs already spread, she said:

'Don't forget the Parisian – and get those dice beakers off! I have to pay extra for the sheets being laundered.'

'Wouldn't think so to look at the colour of them,' Schulze said without rancour, janking off his boots obediently. 'But get that tit-holder off. I want to have a feel at what I'm paying for. You know what Goethe said – "Feeling is everything"?'

'Screw Goethe! It'll cost you five marks more to feel my tits.'

He tossed a five mark piece on to the little bedside table.

'Great crap on the Christmas tree – and this is what we're fighting for!'

Finally he was naked, but still holding his precious rucksack in his hand, Schmeisser machine-pistol slung over his muscular shoulder.

'Where can I put these?' he asked. 'I don't want anyone nicking them while I'm in the saddle.'

'Do you want me to tell you where to put them?' she said in a bored voice, her eyes still fixed on the ceiling.

'What about the cupboard over there?'

Suddenly the tired whore's voice was animated. She raised her body hastily.

'Not there – I've got my private things in there, soldier!'

'All right,' he said easily. 'Don't wet yer knickers, cheetah.' He dropped the pack and the machine-pistol and pushed them under the sagging bed. 'Now then, get them pearly gates open. Here I come – and it's been a long, long time!'

Schulze was lazily guzzling Holsten beer from the bottle the whore had brought him as she bent over his body trying to rouse him once more, when the sound of heavy, steel-shod boots coming down the corridor disturbed his contentment. He took the bottle from his mouth and listened. The whore, her head close to his loins, continued with her labour of love. Suddenly the harsh stamp of feet stopped. A heavy fist hammered on the door.

'Open up,' an official voice demanded. 'Field Gendarmerie – *open up!*'

The whore started with fear.

'Go away,' Schulze shouted. 'I'm on my honeymoon – I don't want to be disturbed, do you hear—'

His words were drowned by the sound of the door being kicked open. Two chain-dogs stood there, machine-pistols in their big hands, suspicious eyes taking in the little dingy room.

'Police,' the bigger of the two snapped.

'Don't bother to introduce yourself,' Schulze said. 'Just come on in and we'll make up a foursome.'

'You in the SS?' the question came from a cold-eyed man, in the long leather-coat and wide-brimmed felt hat uniform of the Gestapo, who had followed the MPs into the room. He indicated the blood group tattooed on the inside of Schulze's upper arm.

'That's right, the Wotan. And what gives a poor shitty-arsed front-line swine like me the honour of such noble company as yourself and your two toy soldiers there?'

'Shut up,' the cold-eyed Gestapo man snapped. Without permission, he picked up Schulze's stained tunic, automatically noting the breast covered in decorations, and fumbled in the pockets till he had found the soldier's paybook. He tossed it to the bigger of the chain-dogs. The latter glanced through it carefully, then handed it back to the Gestapo man with a shake of his helmeted head.

'Anybody else in here?' he asked in a flat, harsh voice.

'What the hell do you types think I'm giving in here – a fucking exhibition or something!' Schulze exclaimed indignantly.

But even as he said the words, he knew that there was something wrong. The look of absolute fear in the whore's faded eyes told him that; raids like this were an everyday occurrence in the Herbertstrasse. Why should she be so scared? The Gestapo man ignored the remark.

'Have a look in that cupboard, corporal,' he ordered the chain-dog.

'No.' The whore flung herself from the bed with surprising speed, her breasts shivering and thrust herself, naked as she was, in front of the door to the cupboard. 'No,' she cried, 'I've got my private things in there. You've no right to search them.'

'The Gestapo has all the rights,' the civilian said. 'Besides what has a whore got that is private?' he added with a sneer.

The MP Corporal grabbed hold of the woman's arm and tried to force her away. But he was too confident. He did not anticipate what happened next. The woman brought up her knee sharply and crashed it into his crotch. He staggered back gasping, his false teeth bulging from his mouth with the shock and pain of the surprise blow.

'She kneed me,' he yelped unnecessarily. 'The bitch kneed me.'

'Get the whore out of the way,' the Gestapo man ordered angrily. 'We haven't got all day!'

The chain-dog acted swiftly. He brought up the steel butt of his machine-pistol and crashed it into the whore's scarred stomach. She shrieked with pain and sank to her knees.

'Hey, what the hell do you think you're doing. After all she might be a whore, but she's a woman too!' Schulze said hotly, springing from the bed.

'Hold yer water,' the Gestapo man cried, his eyes gleaming now, confident that he was on to something, 'or it might be the worse for you! Now get that shitty door open will you—'

'You don't need to,' a youthful voice said as the door was opened from the inside to reveal a pale-faced youth of sixteen or so in the shabby Hitler Youth uniform worn by the Anti-

Aircraft Auxiliaries*. 'And leave my sister alone. She had nothing to do with—'

He did not finish his words. The Gestapo man strode across the little room and slapped him brutally across the face, with a snort of rage.

'Shut that mouth of yours, Hansen, or I'll shut it for you, before you ever reach Neuengamme.'

As the youth slumped against the wall, the Gestapo man slammed his fist deep into his solar plexus. Schulze stared at the strange scene taking place before his eyes in bewilderment. As the two chain-dogs pulled the youth upright, the tears of pain streaming down his deathly pale face, Schulze cried:

'Won't someone tell me what you lot are soddingly well playing at here!'

'Get your clothes on and get out of here, soldier, while the going's good,' the Gestapo man ordered, not turning round to look at the big soldier.

It was unfortunate for him that he did not; for by not doing so, he failed to see the sudden light of resolve beginning to dawn in Schulze's eyes. While the whore got to her feet moaning with pain and the MPs concentrated on their interrogation of the strange pale-faced youth, Schulze raced into his clothes, his mind made up.

'Excuse me,' he tapped the leather-coated Gesgapo man on the shoulder.

'What the hell is it?'

'This!' Schulze smashed the beer bottle across his forehead and he went down without a sound, as if he had been pole-axed.

'You bastard,' the bigger chain-dog roared and leapt at the SS man.

Schulze side-stepped and threw a punch at him. He missed the MP's face and howled with pain as his fist struck the silver plate of office, the MP wore round his neck. The next instant he crashed to the floor, the MP's heavy weight on top of him. Together they rolled back and forth on the floor, each trying to get the upper hand while the whore and the bleeding youth

* Youths, mainly from the Hitler Youth, conscripted into the anti-aircraft defences of most big German cities during the war (*transl.*).

threw themselves on the remaining chain-dog. From down below there was the sound of whistles being blown and the clatter of heavy boots.

Desperately Schulze grabbed hold of the chain-dog's thumb and twisted hard. The man's eyes bulged from his crimson face. He thrust his big hand, palm upwards, under Schulze's chin and pushed with all his strength, trying to break the SS man's hold. Schulze felt himself beginning to black out. A couple of seconds more and he knew he would be gone. Red stars were exploding in the rushing darkness before his eyes. Gasping frantically for air and exerting his last reserves of strength, he twisted. There was a dry snap like that of a twig breaking underfoot. The chain-dog screamed. His body went limp suddenly and the pressure on Schulze's chin eased. The SS man frantically wriggled free. The sound of the heavy boots was coming closer. With a grunt he brought his clubbed fist down on the base of the chain-dog's neck. His spine arched. His head flopped to one side. Schulze had knocked him out completely.

But there was no time to be lost. Gasping painfully, Schulze scrambled to his feet to be confronted by the whore sitting astride the other MP pummelling him with her fists.

'Get that big arse out of the way,' he yelled urgently, 'and let yer father have a go! Aren't you ashamed of showing a great hairy thing like that to an innocent military policeman!'

He shoved her to one side and slugged the remaining chain-dog with his dice-beaker.

'Up here!' a harsh voice yelled in the corridor. 'I tell you I saw the chief come this way!' Apparently someone protested, for the harsh voice repeated. 'By the great whore of Buxtehude, I'm telling you he thought Hansen was up here!'

The naked whore was the first to react.

'Toni,' she cried and pushed him towards the dirty window. 'Out that way. And you too, you great lump! Get that pack of yours – and your popgun – and go with him or the head-hunters!'

She did not need to finish the warning. For once Schulze did not stay and try to be funny. He knew that even his Knight's

Cross would not save him from Torgau* if the chain-dogs caught him now.

'What about you, Gerda?' the pale-faced youth in the shabby black uniform asked urgently.

'Don't bother about me. I'm just a ten-mark whore. It's you, they're after. Go on, get on with it!'

The boy needed no further urging. Hurriedly he opened the window, while Schulze slung his gear over his shoulder. The heavy boots were coming closer. The boy swung himself deftly up and out on to the small brick ledge beyond, followed by Schulze. Below in the evening gloom he could just make out the house's overflowing rubbish dump. It must have been a drop of at least twenty metres.

'Oh, my aching arse,' Schulze breathed. 'I get dizzy even when I stand on a tall chair!'

'Knock it off!' the whore commanded. 'They're here!'

She pulled the window down and drew the blackout curtains. Clinging to the wall, his fingers boring into the eaves, his big boots thrust into the worn brickwork, Schulze could hear the chain-dogs tramp into the whore's room. Questions were barked at her and Schulze heard the sound of a slap.

'Freeze!' the boy next to him hissed urgently.

Schulze squeezed himself even closer to the bricks. The blackout curtain had been flung back. A thin shaft of yellow light sliced into the growing darkness. The next moment the window was thrust open. Schulze caught a half glimpse of a helmeted head peering out. A torch beam cut into the evening and illuminated the overflowing trash cans in the yard below. It swung back and forth for what seemed an eternity to the sweating Schulze. Finally the chain-dog was satisfied.

'Nobody down there,' he reported.

'All right, you take care of the Chief, and I'll see to this sow!' the unknown speaker emphasized his point by slapping the whore again.

Next to Schulze, the boy tensed, but no sound escaped from his tightly clenched lips. The window was shut again and the curtains drawn. The iron-shod boots clattered down the stairs a few minutes later. But still the two men balancing precariously

* The feared Germany Army military prison (*transl.*).

on the narrow ledge did not move until the noisy rattle of the chain-dogs' motorbikes below told them that the danger was over.

'All right,' Schulze said, turning slowly and with some difficulty to face the pale youth, 'now tell me what all that was in aid of, would you?

The boy clenched his fist dramatically and proclaimed in a conspiratorial voice:

'Red Front, comrade ... I'm a member of the communist underground!'

Schulze nearly fell off the ledge.

'Oh, I'll go and piss up my sleeve – what the hell have I let myself in for now?'

THREE

It was the same question that was running through Major Kuno von Dodenburg's mind as he faced Group Leader Schellenberg that afternoon in Madame Kitty's private sitting-room. The blowsy, tough Madame, who dressed as if she were forty, but looked everyday of the seventy she really was, had brought Schellenberg a bottle of his favourite Moselle *Piesporter Goldtroepfchen* and had been inclined to stay. But the youthful head of the SS Secret Service, with his sleek black hair, impudent eyes and cynical mouth, had sent her away.

She went, closing the big double doors behind her slowly, while von Dodenburg gazed around the room. He imagined that this was the way such establishments had looked in the days of the old Imperial Army, with the big-breasted mermaids frolicking in an impossibly blue sea in the Boecklin hanging in its pompous gilt frame on the wall and the Nippes statue, next to his elbow, depicting two gleaming white Amazons doing something anatomically impossible to each other.

'It is Kitty's idea of what constitutes good taste,' Schellenberg said, catching his look and pouring out the white wine. The ex-lawyer's voice was soft and very polite – too polite to be genuine, von Dodenburg could not help thinking. 'But then she has spent all her life in such –er – establishments and there is nothing more respectable than an ex-whore, is there?' He passed von Dodenburg a glass.

'*Prost!*' he brought the glass up level of the third button on his tunic, elbow extended at a right angle to it, as military custom prescribed.

'*Prost!*' von Dodenburg responded.

'Well, Major von Dodenburg, I am sure you are wondering what the Reich Main Security office has to do with an establishment, which, I suppose one could class in the parlance of the man-in-the-street, as a whorehouse, eh?' He smiled and sipped his wine carefully.

'Somewhat.'

'You could say that I started my official career here when my old chief General Heydrich thought he would take a leaf out of Stieber's* book and open a discreet little establishment, catering for all types of sexual pleasure among those who one might classify as – high society. We modernized the Stieber concept of course. Our girls – and boys, we must concern ourselves with that particular one too – are all trained members of the SD, speaking two foreign languages, and each room is wired to the central listening system in the cellar.' He saw the look in the young officer's eyes. 'Oh, yes, every word, each groan, any perverse little desire is being recorded at this very moment beneath our feet.' He chuckled. 'What a treasure chest our records would be for a blackmailer, eh! Ciano, Ribbentrop, Goering – they have all been here, though the good Reich Marshal was not very effective, I can tell you. Yes, my dear Major, I really learned about life in the good Kitty's establishment—'

'But, sir,' von Dodenburg cut in, a little irritated by the smart young SD chief's loquacity. 'I can't really see what all this has got to do with me.'

'Of course, all that was by way of a preliminary. In short, what I wanted to say was, I have listened long enough. Now the time has come for action.'

'What kind of action?'

Schellenberg tapped the ends of his long, well-manicured fingers together. 'In essence, von Dodenburg, the problem is whether we can rely upon you to support Colonel Geier in his direction of the Wotan when the time is ripe.'

'Who is we and what is the time, sir?'

Schellenberg took a careful sip of his Moselle.

'Let me answer the second question first. We lawyers, von Dodenburg, are very fond of the oblique approach, I'm afraid. Well, in any period of internal crisis, we feel there ought to be certain troops like yours – elite formations, which can be relied upon to help to solve that crisis. In Berlin we have the Guards Battalion, for instance; In Poland the Greater Germany Division; in Italy your own Wotan – all units located in strategic places throughout the Reich and the occupied territories.'

* Head of the Prussian Secret Police in the nineteenth century.

'And the we, Group Leader?' von Dodenburg persisted.

'Ah, the we,' Schellenberg looked hard at von Dodenburg. 'Well, I could tell you they are certain key officers of the Wehrmacht, the Armed SS and naturally my own service.'

'You're talking in circles, Group Leader,' von Dodenburg snapped, growing angry as well as apprehensive at Schellenberg's procrastination. 'You haven't answered my question.'

'Naturally,' Schellenberg said without offence. 'I'd risk my head if I did.' He paused momentarily. 'And that of your good father.'

'*My father!*' von Dodenburg gasped.

'Yes, after all, he was one of the instigators of the whole affair. Now he is a key member of our organization in your native East Prussia.'

'To do what?'

'Well, in essence, we must take certain action if the Führer will not make peace before it is too late.'

'And that action?' von Dodenburg rapped.

'*To overthrow Adolf Hitler!*'

'Wagner!' Schellenberg shouted, finally breaking the shocked silence which greeted his announcement.

The big doors opened immediately to reveal Wagner stuffing back his pistol into its holster. He grinned at von Dodenburg's look.

'Just a precaution, Major, just a precaution.'

'Is General von Dodenburg on the line, Wagner?'

'Yessir and spitting blood too because I made him wait.' He looked at von Dodenburg. 'Your father is an exceedingly hot-tempered man. He threatened to come up to Berlin personally and whip my arse if I didn't hurry up.'

'Come,' Schellenberg ordered, 'the scrambler's in the other room.'

They passed into another ornate and vulgar room where a green telephone receiver lay on the table next to a painting of the sexual act, which looked as if it had been painted in the previous century.

'I am sure your father would have no objection to my listening to the conversation,' the SD man said. 'I'm sure you won't either.' He did not wait for confirmation but picked up the attachment.

'Certainly.'

Von Dodenburg picked up the phone.

'Is that you, Kuno?' his father's voice exploded in his ear; the old man could never get used to the idea that one did not need to shout to be heard over the telephone.

'Yes, Father.'

'And damned time too, Kuno. I want to speak to you, naturally, but I am also in great need of an opportunity to pass water. You know the state of my damned outside plumbing?'

Kuno von Dodenburg did. It resulted from 'living well but not too wisely', as the old General was wont to bark whenever the doctor had to be called to deal with the problem. In spite of the gravity of the situation he smiled, and imagined the old man sitting on his old regimental saddle in the dark library, filled with the dusty tattered momentoes of ten generations of his family's service in the cause of the Hohenzollerns* and what came thereafter: the tattered old flag which had flown at Bluecher's side at Waterloo; the large ornate chandelier looted at Metz in '70; the great sword a remote ancestor had wielded for the Great Elector; the letter under glass which had been written to a von Dodenburg by Old Fritz – a score of items proving the von Dodenburgs' loyalty to their masters. And now that family was preparing to betray its leader for the very first time.

'The East is lost,' his father was saying matter-of-factly. 'At night we already can hear the guns here. The Reds have proved better than us. They have transformed their country into a perfectly organized inhuman ant-heap producing more guns, tanks, soldiers than we can ever do. Soon the Red tide will overrun us, if we don't do something to stop it now.'

Kuno von Dodenburg attempted a joke.

'Well, you've got your defences organized in the estate, haven't you, Father?'

'Naturally I won't be taken personally without a fight. After all I am – I was – a soldier. But that is not what I meant. We cannot stop the Reds militarily any more. That is obvious. We

* The Prussian ruling house until 1918.

must do so through a combination of political and revolutionary means.'

Von Dodenburg caught his breath. Now he realized, for the first time, the full extent of what the man standing next to him had planned. 'Revolutionary, what do you mean, Father?'

'Politically, by surrendering what we have taken by force in the East – and in the West naturally – and revolutionary – well, it's self-evident isn't it, Kuno? If your Führer does not agree, then we must get rid of him.'

'How?' Overhearing the contempt in his father's voice, he forced himself to ask the impossible question, 'how will you get rid of him, Father?'

'By force, of course. Wake up, boy – by *force*!' his father snapped testily.

'But that ... that would be rank treason,' he breathed in horror, 'you cannot do that!'

'Of course, it's treason, Kuno, and of course we are playing for high stakes. But it must be done for the sake of our country, even if it means breaking our holy oath as soldiers and von Dodenburgs too.' He paused for breath. 'Are you still there, Kuno?'

'Yes, Father.'

'I must go now, but look after yourself, boy. You are the last von Dodenburg.' Then the phone went dead.

Schellenberg looked across at Kuno von Dodenburg as he took the phone from the pale-faced young officer's hand and replaced it in its cradle, but he said nothing. Wagner spoke for him, the humour gone from his voice now.

'If I may take the liberty of summing up your present situation, Major von Dodenburg,' he said slowly, 'you are faced by two alternatives. You join us and save, not only Germany, but your father's life too, for we shall be found out if we do not act soon. That is obvious. Or you betray us and thus deliver us into the hands of the Gestapo.' He smiled faintly. 'In the language of the front-line swine, my dear Major, we have you truly by the short and curlies, haven't we?'

FOUR

The brother of the whore pushed a glass of weak wartime beer across the stained counter in the smoky little pub opposite the station.

'No good,' he said, hardly opening his lips lest he be overheard by the mixed company of black marketeers, soldiers waiting to catch their trains back and the whores, who filled the place. 'The comrade in the RTO* tells me that they are looking out for you at the barriers.'

'It's my handsome mug,' Schulze answered, taking a swig at the beer and pulling a face. 'Once seen, forgotten for ever.'

'But you must be serious,' the boy said. 'Your life is at stake. They take our comrades to Neuengamme Concentration Camp for less than what you have done this day.'

'You and your shitty comrades,' Schulze growled. 'Can't you call them mates or something?'

In his heart, he knew the boy was right. He had struck a chain-dog and floored a Gestapo man; and if that weren't bad enough, he had helped a bolshevik to escape. They would have the bollocks off him for that.

'But all I wanted to do was to get the dirty water off my chest and then go and see my old man out in Barmbek.'

'There is no question of doing that now,' the pale-faced boy said with the assurance of a man twice his age. 'They have your description and the fact you belong to the SS. You must get out of the Reich and back to your unit at the front as soon as possible. There you'll be safe.'

Schulze looked incredulously at him through the smoky haze.

'Safe at the front – that I don't laugh! They're killing people out there, you know.'

'I know,' the boy answered gravely. 'But believe me, far worse things than death are happening back here in the Reich. Out at Neuengamme, they are torturing people to death slowly,

* Rail Transport Office (*transl.*).

very slowly, by means which you cannot even imagine. That's why we must strike at the fascist beasts soon before they have killed the best of the comrades. We *must* get rid of them.'

Schulze thought of the many millions of Germans, who blindly served the National Socialist cause and told himself the boy was living in a dream world; he and his 'comrades', whoever they might be, would never make the man in the street turn against Hitler until it was too late.

'You might be right, but at this particular moment, sonny, I'm worried about Mrs Schulze's boy. You got me into this mess, how about getting me out of it?'

The young communist's grave face brightened.

'Don't worry, comrade, we'll get you out of Hamburg and back to your unit all right. Tell me first, where you have to return to?'

Schulze quickly filled in the details, while around him the dark-eyed whores screamed hysterically on the soldiers' knees and the black marketeers exchanged their wares surreptitiously under the beer-stained tables.

'Good,' the boy said finally, 'we shall see that you meet your officer at the *Lehrter Bahnhof* by four o'clock tomorrow afternoon. I think we'd better go and see Fat Erna. It looks as if she could pull off the wounded soldier routine with you.'

'And who's Fat Erna when she's at home?' Schulze asked, finishing off his beer.

For the first time since Schulze had met him in the Herbertstrasse, the boy's face broke into a smile.

'You'll see, comrade. All I can say at the moment is that she's a helluva lot of woman.'

Fat Erna was washing her enormous bulk in a chipped enamel bowl in front of the green-tiled stove when they opened the door of her room. Schulze's mouth dropped open at once. Fat Erna, who must have weighed well over a hundred kilos, was completely naked save for a tiny white washcloth with which she was rubbing her left breast, as if she were kneading dough for the oven.

'Christ on a crutch!' he breathed, 'I haven't seen so much fresh meat since the days before rationing!'

'Shut the shitty door,' the big blonde woman growled, 'there's a draught. Or have you got sacks out there!'

Hastily Schulze did as she ordered. Fat Erna dropped the cloth into the grey water with a splash and began to pummel herself with a towel, sizing the SS man up as she did so.

'Well, don't stand there like a spare dildo in a convent!' she snapped finally. 'You'd think you'd never seen a naked woman before. Give me that robe on the chair there!'

Schulze handed the flowered silken kimono to her and while she slipped it on, glanced round her room. Despite the fact that the house was located in Hamburg's poorest working-class district Rotenburgsort, not far from the bombed shunting yards, it was a virtual treasure chest. Cans of coffee were stacked everywhere. One wall was nearly hidden in the brown woollen blankets that would have brought a fortune on the black market, if they could have been sold to those shabby Hamburg housewives who turned such blankets into coats. And the only piece of decent furniture in the room, an enormous double bed was piled high with cartons of American cigarattes, captured on some front or other.

The boy caught his look.

'Subscriptions from our workers,' he said proudly, 'sacrificed to help the cause.'

'Pinched on the trains, you mean,' the enormous woman growled, coiling her long blonde hair into tight plaited snails above her ears. 'And I bet they only gave us half of what they pinched, the bastards.'

'You're a cynic, Erna.'

She poked a tobacco-stained finger like a sausage at her enormous bosom and snorted.

'If you'd have been as long in the Movement as I have, laddie, you'd be a cynic too. You know what Comrade Lenin said about the German working classes – they'd always be too scared to step on the lawn to start a revolution . . . You and your workers, you've still got eggshell behind your ears. All right, you don't need to look at me like that. I'm a realist that's all. Now then, what do you want me to do with that?' she jerked a thumb in Schulze's direction.

Schulze opened his mouth to tell her he didn't fancy her

doing anything with him, but decided against it. He closed his mouth again and let the boy do the talking; it might be safer.

The youngster hurriedly explained the situation, while the fat woman listened in silence, puffing at a thin black cigar. Finally she turned and stared at Schulze, as if she were trying to read his mind.

'All right,' she said in the end. 'I'll have a go at it. Now listen – and listen carefully to what I'm going to say.' Again she poked her sausage-like finger at the big white right breast which kept escaping from her gown every time she moved, as if it led an independent life from the rest of her body.

'All right, I'll play my Sister Klara role. You've got a head wound.' She tapped her forehead. 'You haven't got all your cups in your cupboard any more – it shouldn't be too difficult for you to play that role. You don't look too swift in the upper storey as it is. Anyway, I'm taking you to Professor Sauerbruch, the surgeon at the Charité Hospital in Berlin, to see if he can clear away the cobwebs in your big wooden nut.'

'But if they're looking for me at the railway station, won't the chain-dogs recognize my big handsome mug?' Schulze protested.

Fat Erna shook her head in disgust so that her whole enormous body shook.

'It just goes to show how thick you SS men are! You'll have a flaming bandage round it, won't you, if you've had a head wound! We'll fix it so that even your stupid mother won't recognize it.'

'But even then I'll need papers.'

'You ask too many questions, soldier,' the boy interjected. 'But you have risked your life to help me and I must help you.' His voice rose fervently. 'We have comrades everywhere these days, waiting for the day when the reckoning with the fascists begins—'

Schulze gave one of his celebrated farts and brought the lecture on revolutionary principles to a sudden end. The boy glared at him and the big SS man said:

'I'm sorry, son, it just slipped out like that.'

'Yes,' the fat woman butted in, 'and let that be the only thing that slips out. I know you shitting SS men. I'm not having you trying to get your hand up my skirt or having a fly feel at my tits. Because if you try it on, I'll have your hand off smartish. Understand, soldier?' she growled.

Schulze gulped. 'Yes, I understand, miss,' he said meekly.

'All right then, this is the way we're going to pull it off . . .'

'You understand, von Dodenburg,' Wagner said easily after Schellenberg had gone, 'that I shall have to keep an eye on you till you meet that man of yours and fly off with your popguns? I hope you don't mind. But I think it is in everybody's interests.'

Von Dodenburg nodded morosely and sipped at the *Kron* which Kitty had just brought in. He did not say anything; his mind was too full of his father's words on the telephone. They were going to get rid of the Führer – 'by force', his father had said.

'Don't look so glum, Major,' Wagner said cheerfully, a little flushed from the schnapps. 'We've got to spend the night together, so we might as well enjoy ourselves. Though I must confess to you that after working in this place on and off for the last couple of years, my tastes have become – how shall I put it – rather refined.'

'What do you mean?' von Dodenburg asked dully, his speech beginning to slur a little with the fiery spirit.

'What about having a look?' The big black-uniformed adjutant, who, as von Dodenburg now knew, kept tabs on Himmler for Schellenberg, reached over easily and pressed the bell on the table.

Kitty appeared almost immediately, her face freshly roughed, her lips bright scarlet, ready for the evening's customers.

'Yes, Hans-Werner?'

'Are they there?'

'They're there, Hans-Werner, but—' she hesitated.

'But, what?' Wagner bellowed. 'They've come, haven't they? So they know what they're shittingly well here for!'

'I know, but they are – so young.' The brothel owner's eyes flashed across to von Dodenburg as if she might find support there, but von Dodenburg's mind was too occupied with the question: *what should he do?*

'So what, they've all got to start somewhere. Shit on the Christmas tree, Kitty, you should know that! And what's the difference between them and your trained performing seals – it's tighter, that's all. Go on, woman, bring them in!'

The first girl came through the big doors boldly, her budding breasts thrust out provocatively. The second girl, clad like the first in the black and white uniform of the Union of German Maidens, was just as pretty, but hesitant, almost fearful so that Kitty had to give her a gentle push and propel her into the room.

For a moment the five of them stood there awkwardly: Kitty, the pandar; Wagner, his eyes running up and down the girls' slim young bodies with naked hunger; von Dodenburg, puzzled and nervous; and the two girls neither of whom looked a day over fourteen, the willing and the unwilling victims. Wagner was first to break the silence.

'Well, von Dodenburg, didn't I say that my tastes were rather – er – refined? All right, Kitty, you've done your duty, now you can get back to your performing seals.' He grinned, not taking his eyes off the first girl with the provocative breasts tilting through the thin material of her white uniform blouse. 'There is a war to be won, even in Salon Kitty isn't there?'

The black-clad Madam hesitated, then she shrugged slightly and closed the big doors behind her.

'Come, my little rabbit,' Wagner said, crooking his finger at the first Maiden, 'come and sit on my knee. Uncle won't hurt you.'

The girl giggled and came forward willingly enough, as if she were only too eager to get on with it and have it over and done with. She sat down carelessly on his knee, the short black skirt riding up her bare legs to reveal the simple white panties below. Wagner placed his hand over her breast. She giggled again and made a half-hearted attempt to push his hand away.

'Come on, Heidi.' she simpered. 'Don't let the officer wait.'

She indicated von Dodenburg, who knew now what Wagner meant by his 'refined' tastes. Heidi, a pale blonde with serious blue eyes, came forward hesitantly; then with a visible effort of will sat herself on his knee.

'That's the way,' Wagner roared, pleased with the two girls' reactions, and handed his girl a drink. 'Come on, my little rabbit. Drink up. The night may be cool!'

Again the Maiden giggled and seizing the glass, emptied it in one go. Wagner pretended amazement.

'That is what the Führer means by total war, von Dodenburg!' he gasped. 'Even the youngest folk comrade can empty a glass of schnapps in no seconds! Here, little rabbit, have another one.'

'Do you want one?' von Dodenburg asked the girl on his lap.

She shook her head. Her thin hand touched the medals on his stained grey tunic.

'Knight's Cross, Silver Wound Medal, Combat Infantry Badge, you have them all, Major, you must be a very brave man?'

He laughed softly despite his mood.

'You know all about medals and you a girl?' he asked.

Her beautiful face grew serious.

'In our home evenings* we learn all about medals, Major. The Youth Group Leader says it is important to know what our brave soldiers are giving their blood for.'

'So you think it's medals that soldiers fight for?' he asked. 'But don't answer that question, please. Tell me why you are here instead?'

'I'll tell you, von Dodenburg,' Wagner butted in a little breathlessly, taking his hand from beneath the other Maiden's skirt, and winking. 'Because these two darlings feel that they must do something for their Fatherland and the brave men – *us* – who sacrifice their everything for it. In their turn they are prepared to sacrifice a little thing for us, aren't you, dear?' he squeezed his girl's waist.

With his free hand, Wagner raised his glass.

'Come on, von Dodenburg, drink. Time is short and art is long. Live a little!' He lowered his voice, his bottom lip wet and gleaming. 'Don't they appeal to you like me? Those little breasts, that faint thatch down there – so nice, and clean and unspoiled—'

* Regular compulsory meetings for members of the Union of German Maidens which took place after school or work (*transl.*).

'Pig!' his girl cried and pulled his glass towards her lips.

'Drink, my darling,' he yelled uproariously. 'But I'm not a pig. That Yid Heine knew what he was talking about when he wrote, 'Thou art like a flower, so beautiful, so loyal, so pure.'

'Oh, shut up, Captain,' his girl said and drained the glass. 'Pure indeed – I was brought up in Berlin–Wedding*. There's not much pure there, I can tell you.'

Wagner laughed delightedly.

'Do you see what I mean, von Dodenburg? How deliciously corrupt. A child-whore, spoiled at fourteen. But what does it matter? How beautiful and innocent she is, despite what already has been up that delightful skirt.'

The next instant Wagner had lifted her into his arms, as if she were no weight at all. Rising effortlessly to his feet, but swaying a little with the drink, he stumbled to the door. There he paused and fumbled to open it with one hand, while the girl clung to his neck, her skirt thrown back to reveal her white smooth legs, giggling stupidly. He took one last look at von Dodenburg and the red-faced girl on his knee. Then with the heel of his gleaming jackboot he crashed the door closed behind him.

Von Dodenburg had taken her cruelly and violently, aware that her screams and struggle were both genuine and specious, feeling as he did so that she, too, was like the world all around him; already rotten, heading for corruption and putrefaction.

Afterwards she had not cried, but lain there moaning, as if he had inflicted actual physical pain upon her. But he had no mercy; in that moment he had almost hated her. He had pressed his hand up between her smooth young legs and touched the heated crevice between them again. She had gasped with fear and wriggled her child's hips to try to free herself. She had screamed and he had clapped his hand over her mouth and while she had struggled like a wild animal trying desperately to free itself from a trap, he had thrust himself upon her once more.

The third time he had tormented her, changing his position over and over again, preventing himself from achieving an

* Tough, working-class area (*transl.*).

orgasm, pressing her thin legs high above her head and ploughing her body furiously until she, too, began to feel pleasure and desire. She bit his shoulder and even in his pain, he felt a sense of awareness that she, too, was corrupt now like the whole of Germany was corrupt – like the Reichsführer, Schellenberg, Geier, Wagner, even his own father.

He felt no pleasure, just rage at the injustice of it all. Heidi had experienced a kind of frenzy. Screaming and biting she had writhed back and forth frighteningly, as if she were now riding him and not the other way around, her mouth open, her lips gleaming, uttering obscenities – learned God knows where. And then suddenly she had arched her spine, stopping in the middle of a wild movement, digging her nails into his buttocks so that it hurt and had screamed through gritted teeth,

'Oh, shit . . . shit . . . shit . . .'

Now as the clock struck midnight somewhere, he watched her exhausted face in the silver darkness of the moonlight pouring through the unblacked-out window, silence everywhere save for the persistent squeak of bedsprings somewhere else in the brothel, and felt his rage change slowly to sadness. For this immature girl, who had sacrificed herself to him because he was one of 'our brave soldiers'; for himself, because he knew now that he, too, had been betrayed; for all the honest people in Germany who were still working, sacrificing, fighting and dying in vain for a once great cause that had already sold out behind their backs. The hours passed leadenly. At about two a siren began to sound in the far-off suburbs. A couple of searchlight beams sliced into the night sky and began to probe the silver darkness. But the Tommy raiders they expected did not appear and they flicked off again after a while. And still he could not solve his problem.

He tossed and turned and tried to get to sleep, attempting to force the issue out of his mind. But the problem simply would not go away. He could not betray his father, that he knew. But he could not also betray his Führer and Fatherland. What in heaven's name was he going to do?

Dawn came, harsh, grey and wintery, a typical Berlin morning. But even its cold greyness could not impair the guilelessness of the girl's sleeping face. Her lips were opening and closing now, as if she were thirsty. He bent down and pressed a kiss on them softly. Her breath was sweet. She stirred slightly, but did not wake. He put his hand gently on her breast and massaged the nipple gently. It began to grow erect under his touch.

Slowly her legs arched and began to part. The covers slipped away from her stomach and he could see the smooth white curve of her thighs, decorated by the dark pubic puff. Cautiously he placed his other hand on her stomach. She did not stir. He let it glide down the white slope. He hesitated. She looked so childishly innocent that he felt himself choke. But there is no more innocence he told himself harshly. His fingers slipped into the dark hair. Her breath began to come more rapidly. Rhythmically her buttocks commenced moving up and down, slowly at first, but growing ever quicker as he increased his fondling.

Suddenly her eyes flickered open. For a moment he could see that she did not understand what was happening to her, who he was and where they were. Then her thin arms groped round his neck and her mouth opened for him to kiss her. As he bent to do so, she parted her legs expectantly. He raised himself and pressed his hands under her firm buttocks.

'Wider,' he gasped, feeling lust overcome him now.

He lowered himself carefully between the white cradle of her legs. She grunted as his weight descended upon her, the grunt turning into a gasp, whether of pain or pleasure, von Dodenburg neither knew nor cared in his excitement. Brutally and pleasurably he thrust himself inside her. Her loins writhed up to meet him, as if her body could not receive enough of him.

'*Good . . .oh, good,*' she quavered, and let it happen once again.

Two hours later, Wagner was hammering on the door, naked save for his polished jackboots and the revolver belt around his waist. One arm was clasped around the other girl, who was swaying drunkenly, long hair dangling over her face. In his other hand, he held a bottle of champagne and four glasses.

'Ah, ah, Major von Dodenburg,' he chortled, as von Dodenburg opened up for him and he saw the girl stretched naked and exhausted on the rumpled bed, 'frolicking with little girls, eh? Don't you know, sir, that that is a punishable offence in our brave new National Socialist Germany?' He grinned. 'Come on Kuno, Madame Kitty is going to give us a champagne breakfast – real French champus too. None of your Saar muck–'

It was then that von Dodenburg punched him very neatly on the jaw. As the glasses fell to the floor and the big adjutant swayed backwards, taken off his guard completely, the Wotan officer followed up his punch with a swift kick to Wagner's genitals which sent him smashing to the wall. Ignoring the screaming girls and the big naked SD man with the vomit trickling from his wildly gasping mouth, slowly sliding down the wall, von Dodenburg picked up his clothes and equipment. His mind was made up at last.

FIVE

'All right,' Big Erna hissed, as they crouched together in the little copse of pines overlooking the suburban station of Reinbek, 'now pin back your big ears and listen to what I'm going to say because I'm only going to say it once. Right?'

'Right?' Schulze whispered, half amused, half impressed by this monstrous woman who was risking her life to get him back to Berlin.

'The hospital train gets in from the front punctually at midnight. Then the headhunters will seal off the platform down there and the barriers to the street, in case any civvie who might be about still sees the wounded being unloaded. The powers-that-be naturally do not want their folk comrades to see the mess they are making of the fighting on the Russian front. But I don't need to tell you that, Schulze, you've been there, haven't you?'

'That I have, missus. I've been there twice and I've had a noseful.'

'Morc fool you,' she grunted. 'It's thick-headed fools like you with their brains between their legs who keep the imperialists in power. But no matter now. The train will leave for Hamburg, take on leave men returning to the front and a new hospital crew. Of course there'll be a check at Hamburg, but no one will suspect that we will be aboard. So', she took a hasty glance at the luminous dial of her watch, raising it up to the moon's beams: 'as soon as we're aboard, head for the other rank latrines at the far end and stay in there till we've left Hamburg Main Station. Clear?'

'Clear. Just one thing, though.'

'Yes?' she said impatiently.

From up the line there came the faint steady puffing of a heavily laden train. On the platform, the blue lamps were beginning to light up and there was the sound of heavy military boots.

'How are we going to get off when the train stops again in Berlin? There must be a check there.'

Big Erna laughed softly this time with genuine mirth.

'Sister Klara has got an answer for that one, soldier. Never fear. Look.'

With considerable speed for such an enormous woman, she flipped up the back of her loose white nurse's skirt to reveal a brief glimpse of great buttocks, covered by tightly stretched sheer black panties.

'That'll be all the documents you'll need, take it from me,' she said mysteriously. 'Now shut up, here comes the hospital train.'

'Well, all I can say is that I wouldn't like to buy all that by the kilo,' Schulze whispered, his eyes fixed on the white-painted train which was now beginning to pull into the little station.

With a rusty squeal of brakes and emitting a great cloud of steam, the white-painted locomotive came to rest at the end of the platform. For a moment nothing happened. Then the stretcher-bearers started to file on the platform, pushing their way through the MPs armed with sub-machine guns who were watching the streets. The young Red Cross nurses hurried out of the blue-lit waiting-room, shivering in the night cold, their knives and scissors held ready in their hands. The doors of the train were flung open everywhere and now the two watchers could identify the strange sound which had puzzled them ever since the locomotive had stopped.

'It's the wounded,' Fat Erna hissed. 'They've been locked up in that train for three days, ever since it left the front. You can imagine the state of the poor bastards, can't you?'

Schulze did not need to; he could see their state with his own eyes, as the ragged, lice-ridden soldiers were laid out in long rows on the freezing platform while the nurses went down their moaning ranks slicing their lousy, blood-stained clothes with professional speed. They were followed by elderly soldiers with masks over their mouths, pumping great clouds of lice-powder over their naked, broken bodies.

'Against typhus,' Fat Erna explained. 'There was a typhus epidemic out here last year, but the authorities hushed it up – as always.' She gave a last quick look at the platform and nudged Schulze. 'All right, soldier boy, let's go!'

Schulze needed no urging. Together they scrambled down the steep wooded slope, Fat Erna showed surprising energy and agility for such a big woman and, crouching low, clambered over the gleaming rails towards the train.

'Towards the rear,' she hissed. 'It's darker there – behind that flak wagon.'

Hurriedly, but taking care not to make too much noise, they worked their way past the stark outline of the Luftwaffe anti-aircraft car, its four 20mm cannon pointing mutely to a silver night sky. Erna stopped suddenly, so that he nearly bumped into her.

'This is it – the dysentery latrines.'

'Yeah, I can smell them! Christ on a crutch! That pong certainly makes yer hair curl, doesn't it?'

'By the time you get out of them, soldier,' Big Erna said grimly, 'your hair will probably have started to fall out. All right, once you're in them, stay there until we cross the bridge over the Elbe at Lauenburg. Got it?'

'Got it.'

'Good, now give me a leg up to the carriage – and no trying to get your big hand up my skirt when you do, do you hear?'

'A gentleman never takes advantage of a lady in a tricky situation, madam, especially when she's as big as you.'

Big Erna mouthed an obscenity and reached upwards.

'I shall have to speak first with my chaplain before I can answer that,' Schulz said and took the strain, pushing at her enormous buttocks, as if he were back in the Hamburg docks heaving up hundredweight sacks of flour.

The corridor leading to the dysentery latrines, marked by the big official sign 'ATTENTION DYSENTERY PATIENTS ONLY, was empty, but the bloody mixture of faeces and dirty linen which littered the floor showed clearly that the latrines had been in full use in the hospital train's long journey from the front. Further up, an orderly was sluicing down the floor with a stirrup pump attached to a pail of water.

Big Erna coughed thickly.

'All right, soldier. Now you're on your own. Sister Klara

must get some rest for the long journey back to the front.'

'Lucky you,' Schulze grumbled, then he turned and began to make his way towards the latrine area, already beginning to gag at the nauseating odour which rose to meet him.

Big Erna faced him on the rattling, swaying connection between the two carriages. The noise was so loud that the frozen-faced air-raid sentry in the little wooden tower above their heads could not hear a word they spoke. Outside it was snowing hard – thick white flakes coming down in solid sheets as if God had decided to blot out the miserable war-torn world below for good. Big Erna handed him the little bottle of *Kron.*

'Clean your mouth out with that,' she ordered gruffly.

Gratefully he took a deep drink of the fiery, clear schnapps.

'Man, that tastes good,' he gasped, wiping his cracked lips with the back of his hand. 'I thought I was going to lose my ring in that bog for good – I puked that much.'

'Better than losing your turnip'* she commented laconically and watched the flat white Mecklenburg countryside flash by.

Feeling better now, Schulze looked at the big woman in the Red Cross uniform curiously. 'You been inside?' he asked. She nodded and took a bite of the sandwich she had pulled out of her pocket.

'Is that why you're working with that lad in Hamburg?'

She swallowed a big chunk of the black bread and salami.

'I suppose so. I'm not in the movement because of the ideology, that's for sure. The Party's philosophy is still bourgeois, you know. Not much better than the old anti-feminist business of children, kitchen and cooking. Our leaders haven't much time for the kind of – er – weakness I'm addicted to.'

She lowered her eyes with unusual shyness. Schulze did not ask what her 'weakness' was. He knew Fat Erna well enough now to realize that she would only tell him what she wanted to tell him.

'I'm in this,' she said slowly, taking another bite of her sandwich, as if her very life depended upon her swallowing it, 'be-

* Concentration camp slang for the head (*transl.*).

cause I hate the Nazis, oh God, how I hate the bastards! I'd give my very life to bring them down.'

Still Schulze did not speak. Up above them the anti-aircraft guard removed his leather face mask and wiped the sweat off his brow. His face was young and pale; more cannon fodder to feed the Russian front's insatiable appetite, Schulze thought. The boy smiled down at them and then replaced the leather mask hastily as the full force of the icy, snow-laden wind struck him.

'They took me in in 1934' She stuffed the rest of her sandwich into her mouth. 'I'm a pervert you know.' She laughed bitterly. 'What else could I be – the way I'm built? No man would ever look at me.'

Schulze looked at her in amazement.

'Do you mean?' he stuttered. She grinned at him cynically. 'I do! All my life I've never let one of you male pigs up my drawers. At first I hated you because you men despised me for my size. Later I began to look at you in contempt. After all,' she pulled another black bread sandwich out of her pocket and began stuffing it into her mouth, as if Schulze might take it from her, 'I can do things to women with these hands that you could never hope to do with that dirty little thing you've got hanging in your trousers.'

'Don't say that, Erna,' Schulze protested, 'what do you think I've got these round shoulders for!'

But he could see his humour was out of place. Big Erna's mind was on other times and other places; he was just a sounding board for her memories.

'Funnily enough, the Nazis did me a favour when they sent me to Dachau. I met Elli there – the one great love of my life. And they killed her when they found out. Those Nazi pigs killed her. No gas chamber, no firing squad, no executioner's axe – no, nothing as clean and simple as that for my poor beautiful Elli.' She looked at Schulze, her eyes blazing with sudden hate. 'Do you know what the bastards said? If a man's tail couldn't satisfy her – that was after six of them had been through her – then they'd see what a—' She broke off suddenly.

When she spoke again, she was the old Fat Erna again, completely assured and in control of herself.

'They stuck something up her. I could hear her screams right on the other side of the homo block. Then they left her to bleed to death – *slowly*.'

She said the words without any emotion, fumbling in her pocket for yet another black bread sandwich.

'She was the only person I ever really loved. Now can you understand why I hate them?'

The big SS man nodded silently and looked at the driving snowflakes, burying the winter countryside under their white cruel mantle.

'What a rotten world, it is,' he told himself bitterly, 'what a rotten shitty world.'

Slowly the big hospital train started to steam into the platform, crowded with morose pale-faced soldiers returning to the front and their sobbing wives, watched everywhere by helmeted chain-dogs ready to stamp out any sign of trouble.

The train came to a halt and the wives and girl-friends sobbed into their handkerchiefs with renewed energy, while their menfolk made embarrassed 'tut-tutting' noises. High above them in the shattered glass roof, the loudspeakers came to life:

'Special troop train for Koenigsberg, with connections to Warsaw, Brest–Litovsk, Smolensk, will be leaving Platform Four. Planned departure fifteen hours, forty-five.' The soldiers started to pick up their rucksacks, engulfed in steam and smoke. 'Good luck', the women cried with mounting hysteria. 'Good luck, Willi . . . Good luck, Karl! Now don't forget to look after yourself like I said . . .'

'All right,' Big Erna whispered as the soldiers began to enter the train, pushing their kit and weapons in front of them. 'Now's the time. Walk behind me. When I drop this (she indicated her shabby briefcase) jump the barrier, head into the crowd and run like hell!'

'And you, Erna?'

'Don't worry about me, soldier,' she said gruffly, 'I've got papers. I've nothing to fear.'

He held out his big hand.

'All right, if you say so . . . Thanks for everything you done for me.'

She took it in a fist that was as hard and firm as his own.

'Don't mention it, soldier. At least, you didn't try to put your hand up my skirt – which is more than I can say for the rest of them.'

Schulze simpered.

'Well, you see I don't really like girls.'

She gave him a playful push that nearly sent him through the open door.

'Get on with you. All right now, let's go. Time's running out.'

Hastily she pushed her way through the soldiers crowding around the door.

'Make way there,' she commanded imperiously. 'I've got a seriously wounded man with me. Sauerbruch himself is going to operate on him.'

The name of Germany's greatest surgeon worked like magic. They fell back on both sides to let her emerge, followed by Schulze trying to look seriously wounded. A fat housewife sobbing into a damp handkerchief did not get out of Erna's way quickly enough and the big woman gave her a hefty shove.

'Get out of the road, will you,' she growled, 'you silly sow, or I'll really give you something to cry about.'

The barrier, guarded by two chain-dogs and a civilian who was obviously a member of the Gestapo or Secret Field Police, was only fifteen metres away now. Fat Erna walked towards it purposefully, as if she hadn't a care in the world, fumbling in her briefcase, apparently looking for her pass to show to the guards. Schulze followed at five metres distance, holding his hand to the side of his bandaged face. Suddenly big Erna dropped her briefcase on to the platform, scattering the contents everywhere.

'*Holy shit!*' she cursed loudly so that everyone turned to look at her, 'the sodding thing has come open again!'

With a theatrical grunt she bent down slowly to pick up the contents. Her nurse's skirt rode up her huge flanks to reveal the full glory of her black-silk clad buttocks. At the barrier the chain-dogs' eyes bulged out of their heads at the spectacle. Somewhere close by, a soldier groaned in awe:

'Oh, holy strawsack, get a load of that! All that meat and no potatoes!'

The civilian pulled his dark felt hat down more firmly on his head, as if he were afraid it might be blown off by the shock of the sight being revealed to him and stepped forward.

'Let me give you a hand, sister,' he said hastily, 'before you split your knickers altogether!'

'*Now,*' Big Erna hissed, not looking up. 'And the best of luck, you lump!'

Schulze waited no longer. With one jump he was over the barrier and in the midst of the surprised crowd of shabby civilians waiting for their trains.

'Hey, what's this,' an officious-looking man with a battered case shouted, 'what you think you're up to?'

Schulze gave him a shove in the face, ripping at his bandages with the other hand. The man sprawled full length on the platform. His case burst open. Eggs cascaded on to the ground.

'Black market,' someone shouted. 'Black market eggs!'

The crowd surged forward greedily, attracted by the promise of this luxury. A fat woman slipped on a yolk and careened forward into Schulze, still occupied with his bandage. He jabbed his elbow into her middle and she went down gasping, like a punctured barrage balloon. Schulze pushed on through the chaos.

Behind him the chain-dogs' whistles began to shrill. A red, steel-helmeted face loomed up in front of him. Schulze stopped momentarily and drove his knee into the officer's stomach. The man's knees gave way beneath him like those of a newborn foal. Schulze gave a great guffaw and giving him the slightest of pushes with his right hand, watched him fall on his back.

A severe-looking woman in the grey-green uniform of the 'Belief and Beauty' organization shouted something at him and swung her briefcase. Schulze ducked. The woman overbalanced and Schulze caught her instinctively, his big hands squeezing her breasts.

'Let go,' she gasped in a high-pitched spinster's voice. 'Let go of me!'

'Gladly!' he roared. 'But I bet it'll be the last time somebody'll feel your tits in 1944!' He pushed her to one side. 'Count yourself lucky, missus.'

He ran on, leaving her gasping and protesting in the confused mess of his wake. And then he was outside, the shrill sound of the MPs' whistles and the yells of the crowd getting ever fainter. He flung the bandage into the snow and adjusting his cap, forced himself to walk more slowly towards the front of the station, knowing that if von Dodenburg was not there, he would be sunk.

But Major von Dodenburg was there, standing next to a pale, pretty blonde in Maiden uniform, who hardly came up to his shoulder. He hurried forward, trying to contain his hectic breathing and flung von Dodenburg a tremendous salute.

Von Dodenburg looked at him, his face unshaven, his jacket torn and covered in something which looked like egg-yolk, his Knight's Cross hanging over his shoulder instead of round his neck.

'Heaven, arse, and twine, Schulze,' he roared, 'where the hell have you been? You look as if someone has dragged you through a hedge – backwards!'

And it feels like it too, Schulze told himself, but he did not tell von Dodenburg that. His eyes curiously sizing up the Maiden, he said:

'I was in a hurry to get back, sir.'

'Back to the front?'

Schulze sighed and relaxed.

'Sir, the front will be a rest cure after what has happened to me in the last forty-eight hours.'

Von Dodenburg's grin faded.

'You might be right there, Schulze. The front is preferable to this mess. All right, park your big rear in the car. We're off in a minute.'

He indicated Wagner's Volkswagen jeep which he had simply driven away from Madame Kitty's without the big adjutant's permission, consumed as he had been with a burning rage at the whole miserable state of the Reich and the traitors working so industriously behind the scenes to bring about its downfall. He turned to the girl, who was shivering a little in the cold, and extended his hand formally.

'Well, it's goodbye, Heidi,' he said softly, while Schulze's eyes swept curiously from the oddly matched pair to the exit from the station to check whether the MPs were still after him.

The girl accepted it with the same formality.

'I suppose it is, Mr Major,' she hesitated, opened her mouth as if to say something, then closed it again.

He stroked her straight blonde hair, as if he were patting a small child, not the woman whom he had taken so violently and cruelly that night.

'Look after yourself, Heidi,' he said gently, the rage gone from his voice, now that his mind was made up. 'And don't go back there again – you know what I mean – even if they do tell you that it is your duty to do so. It isn't, you know.'

She nodded mutely. For a moment the two of them stood there in the falling snow, no sound save the soft hiss of the car tyres and somewhere far off the rattle of a tram-bell.

'Shall I see you again, Mr Major?' she asked finally, not daring to look at him.

'No, Heidi, you won't see me again. I shall never come back here now.'

'Then goodbye and happy landings,' she said, raising her face to show that her eyes were full of tears. 'Thank you, Mr Major.'

Major von Dodenburg did not speak all the way to Tempelhof, driving numbly through the winter streets, crowded with pinched scared people hurrying to the shelters because a fresh air-raid warning had sounded. At the airport, he confined himself to a few tense questions to the young pilot of the 'Auntie Ju'* which was going to fly them, complete with recoilless rifles, back to Rome Airport.

It was only when they were airborne and the first of the 8 mm flak started to pepper the grey December sky with black bursts that he ripped open his tunic, slumped deeper in the bucket seat opposite Schulze and uttered a great sigh of relief.

'Thank God, that's the last of Berlin!'

* German Army slang for the three-engined Junkers 52 transport plane (*transl.*).

'Thank God, that's the last of Germany!' Schulze added feelingly. 'The front's simpler for dumb arseholes like me. Down there you've got to have your head screwed on the right way to know who's your friend and who's your foe.'

Von Dodenburg nodded, as the pilot took violent evasive action, swinging the big slow plane out of the way of the first flight of Ami Flying Fortresses gleaming a deadly silver in the harsh sunlight above the cloud base. How right Schulze was. At the front the decisions one had to make were clear-cut and simple. Black and white. None of the corrupting greys of the base stallions.

Now as the transport began to plough its way steadily southwards, Kuno von Dodenburg sat slumped in his seat, his eyes closed, his Fatherland below completely forgotten, his mind completely occupied with a single question, the result of his sudden decision in Madame Kitty's: *when and how would he kill Colonel Geier?*

Three: Battle for the Perimeter

'If you ask me, this is a certain one-way ticket to the little fat-arsed boys with the wings on – a real old Ascension Day commando. '*SS Man Schulze to Major von Dodenburg.*

ONE

Walker's Texans started crossing the Rapido, ten miles east of Peak 555, in the foggy dawn darkness of January 20th, 1944. During the dry season the river was a mere trickle. But after thee months of winter rain and snow the Rapido was a torrent, nine feet deep in some places.

Now the big, confident Texans, laden down with rations, ammunition and weapons, began pushing their clumsy assault boats between the dirty white marker tapes into the water. Still everything was ominously silent.

'Looks okay, Captain, don't it?' Walker said dryly to Captain Pearson, who had been sent down to the river by Clarke to keep the big 5th Army Commander informed of what was going on.

'Looks like it, sir,' he answered, his eyes peering through the haze anxiously.

Once the 36th had managed to get across the river, he knew, they faced four hundred yards of minefields and barbed wire entanglements before they reached the first Kraut positions on the heights beyond. It was not going to be as easy as the Texans thought. The first metal assault boat nosed its way cautiously into the water. Soon the fast-running dark waters of the Italian river were full of them. Here and there the GIs were having trouble trying to keep on course. But most of them were doing well, paddling crazily against the current. Still all was silent on the far bank.

Walker coughed and Pearson started nervously.

'Sorry,' the General apologized, but he didn't take his eyes off the river.

The Texans were almost there now. The observers, grouped round the General, could see the men in the leading boats already putting down their paddles and grabbing their rifles. The first boat hit the mud of the far bank. The Texans were out, splashing through the shallow water. Still nothing happened. Ten yards – five yards and they would be in the minefields. Pearson held his breath. They were going to make the crossing without opposition after all.

Suddenly there was an obscene belch. It was followed by a stomach-churning howl. One – two – three – four – five – six. The first mortar bombs howled through the dirty sky, an angry red.

'Christ on a crutch', a staff officer next to Pearson cursed, 'the screaming meemies!'

As the first shells of the multiple mortar dropped in the water sending up huge, frightening fountains of water, machine-guns opened up everywhere, in response to its signal. Their bullets laced into the first wave of Texans. Bodies piled up on the mudbank. Wounded staggered forward and collapsed in the minefield. Within seconds the whole bank was lined with dead and dying men. They had been cut down before they had been able to fire a single shot.

'My God,' Pearson groaned to himself. The crossing was going to be sheer slaughter.

Walker swung round at his staff.

'Okay, don't stand there like a bunch of goddam dummies,' he snarled, 'get me some artillery support, willya!' The staff officers recovered from their inital shock. The walky-talkies began to crackle.

On the opposite shore the massacre continued. As the shells whizzed dramatically over their heads and smashed into the well dug in Germans on the heights, the latter increased their deadly fire. Red and white tracer swept the whole length of the river. Pearson saw about a dozen Texans running frantically along the mud bank. They still carried their weapons and were firing as they ran to find the cover that wasn't there. One by one they were cut down by the cruel fire and rolled dead to the edge of the water. They were the last of the first wave.

Now the boats filled with dead and dying came drifting back. A skinny private, his eyes wide with shock, his hand clasped to a gaping wound in his shoulder, cried:

'I don't know how it happened!' and staggered by the staff group.

A lieutentant staggered up to Walker his helmet gone, blood pouring down his face, his combat suit grey with mud. Surprisingly enough, he saluted.

'Beg to report, sir, C Company wiped out!' Then his knees gave way and before anyone of the staff officers could catch him, he had dropped next to the boy who had died trying to crawl after him, his right foot clinging to his leg by a shred of skin.

Aghast, Pearson turned to a white-faced Walker and blurted out:

'What are we going to do, sir?'

Walker swung on him angrily: 'What the Sam Hill do you think I'm gonna do, Captain? Your boss asked me to cross the Rapido – and I'm going to do just that.' He turned to one of his majors, whose hands holding the walky-talky were trembling uncontrollably. 'Okay, Holmes, get me the 143rd Infantry.'

A few moments later the second infantry regiment of the 36th Division had been raised and Walker grabbed the instrument from the Major's trembling hands. Ignoring radio procedure, he snapped:

'All right, Colonel, bring up your boys now – the party's in full swing and we need more guests. *Over!*'

The massacre continued. The Texans finally crossed the river, walking across a carpet of their own dead on the far bank. Under the cover of the tremendous Corps artillery bombardment, they battled their way through the minefield and rushed the German positions. Shouting and screaming, they stormed forward.

A machine-gun barked. Its bark became a thin hysterical hiss. Tracer slammed into their massed ranks as the enemy came up out of their deep, cunningly dug holes. Great gaps appeared in the Texans' rank. Here and there, men threw their weapons away and raised their hands in surrender. But death was greedy; it harvested them all the same.

Then it was the Germans' turn. They came out of their holes, as if glad to be released from the tension of crouching and waiting. Armed with bayonets and entrenching tools they went for the survivors, bogged down in the wire and mud. They hacked and kicked. Gouged and throttled with bare hands. When they were finished and had staggered back to their holes, chests heaving, faces pale and sickened, all energy drained out of them, the flattened landscape was olive-drab with the bodies of the boys from Texas.

For a while the battlefield was left to the dead. They lay everywhere in the churned mud: some whole; others spread out among the litter of boots, weapons, field dressings, paper, letters, as if some crazy surgeon had gone to work with explosives instead of a scalpel. Crouched in the mud of the enemy side, waiting for Walker to make up his mind what to do next, Pearson spotted something shining in the mud a few feet away. Almost without thinking, he picked it up. For a moment he thought it was some piece of cheap imitation ivory jewellery that one of the Texans had bought from a Neapolitan backstreet trader. Then he recognized it for what it was: a crescent of human teeth set in a shattered section of human jawbone. As he dropped it with a gasp of horror, Walker spoke wearily into the walky-talky:

'All right, Charley, I guess you'd better bring up your 142nd Infantry now . . . we're in real trouble.'

General Walker was right. By the end of that first day the 26th Infantry Division had taken nearly fifteen hundred casualties. By the end of the second, with the Texans already calling the Rapido 'blood river', the 36th had fought to a standstill and the Division was a shattered wreck.

The Rapido Crossing had been a total disaster. Now it was the turn of the men dug in on top of Peak 555.

2

'Well, gentlemen,' the Vulture rasped, 'it looks as if the stubble-hoppers really gave the Amis a nasty kick in the nuts down there, doesn't it?'

He pointed his riding crop to the thick pall of smoke hanging over the Rapido. Von Dodenburg studiously avoided his look, as he had been avoiding the Vulture ever since he had returned from Berlin, knowing that he would not be able to hold back his burning rage if Geier were to ask him about Schellenberg and the plan. Glumly he looked down the valley through his binoculars, trying in vain to penetrate the smoke.

Otherwise visibility was good and the valley was spread out in front of the watching Wotan officers like a map, each road and track easily identifiable, stretching out like tapes, with roofless farmhouses dotted among the artillery-shattered trees in chessboard fashion. He could see the dark hurrying outlines of Ami trucks bringing up fresh cannon-fodder to thrust into the maw of the hungry beast-of-war waiting on the Rapido. The Amis were obviously getting desperate as the field-greys down below on the river stopped them dead, as though they were pumping in everything they had.

The Vulture must have read his thoughts, for he broke the heavy silence, with:

'As you can see then, the Amis are throwing away their men with the same prodigality as the Ivans did last year when we were at Kursk.* But,' he shrugged slightly, 'they have the men and material. We don't, eh!'

'Yes, sir,' Schwartz said enthusiastically, rising to the bait. 'But one German is worth ten of those Ami gangsters down there. So far their victories have been against inferior people, those yellow-bellied spaghetti-eaters, for instance.' His lips curled in a sneer. 'Now they are fighting Germans.'

'I believe I read somewhere that one in every eight

* Leo Kessler: *Claws of Steel* for further details.

Americans is of German descent, Captain Schwarz,' the Vulture commented mildly.

Out of the corner of his eye, von Dodenburg glimpsed the Creeper reaching for his notebook. The Vulture also spotted the movement:

'Please do not waste any more time writing it down, my dear young Lieutenant,' he said softly. 'If you wish to have – how shall we put it? – written evidence – I will gladly give you my statement in writing later.

'Now I would like you to listen carefully to what I have to say. This morning I was honoured by a direct communication from no less a person than Smiling Albert himself. The Commander-in-Chief stated that he was afraid the Amis would now draw in their heads and lick their wounds after the bloody nose they've been getting down there for the last forty-eight hours.'

'Afraid?' von Dodenburg could not contain his surprise.

'Ah, von Dodenburg, you are with us?' the Vulture looked at him searchingly, pleased that he had drawn a reaction out of the Major at last. 'Yes, afraid was the word – afraid because if they do that, the Führer's great plan might not be realized. And we all know that the great captain of all times does not like his military intentions frustrated.'

'And the plan, sir?' von Dodenburg cut in.

'Ah, yes the great plan. Well, our dear Leader feels that if we cannot achieve a military victory here in Italy, we should at least gain a political and – using the word loosely, very loosely – a moral one.'

As the assembled officers stared at him puzzled, the Vulture swung round and pointed to the grey stone bulk of the Monte Cassino Monastery, set against the tremendous backdrop of the Monte Cairo, soaring two thousand metres into the sky, its rocky gullies streaked with the snow that ran down from its white-capped top.

'It is the Führer's wish that that pile of historical junk should be turned into a ruin. Our pagan forefathers did the job once before a thousand years or more ago, and gained the hatred of the so-called civilized world. Now the Führer wants to ensure that the same business is carried out again – not, however, by the dreadful Germans this time, but by those bearers of liberty and democracy from over the water – the Amis.'

He saw their bewildered looks and smiled thinly.

'Oh, it is very simple, gentlemen. We must provoke the Amis into such a rage that they will destroy the Monastery because they know that it dominates the Liri Valley and is the observation post from which all operations against their lines are directed.'

'But why sacrifice such an ideal observation post, sir,' Schwarz asked.

The Vulture smiled maliciously.

'I think you gentlemen are getting a little soft in the upper storey here on Peak 555. Perhaps it is the mountain air and not enough exercise, eh? Can't you see? If the Amis destroy the "seminal force of Christian civilization in Central Italy", as I believed Baedeker calls the dump—'

'They will be branded as cultural barbarians,' von Dodenburg cut in.

'Yes, von Dodenburg. The destruction of the Cassino Monastery will indicate that the Amis have little regard for our European treasures. The neutral press will have a field day – not to mention our own dear little cripple.'

Even the malicious reference to Dr Josef Goebbels, head of the Reich's Propaganda Ministry, did not spoil their spontaneous enthusiasm as they realized the full subtlety of the Führer's plan.

'Holy straw sack, sir,' young blond-headed Bauer, a new officer in von Dodenburg's battalion, cried. 'How devilishly smart! Only our Führer could think up something like that!'

'Yes, only *our* Führer,' the Vulture agreed.

But in their eagerness to know more, the young officers of the Wotan did not notice his cynicism.

'But how are we going to do it, sir?' someone asked.

'Smiling Albert has given me full instructions,' the Vulture replied. 'He anticipates an Ami withdrawal across the Rapido this evening. The local commander does not believe they will be able to hold out on this bank much longer. As a result, we feel what will happen this evening will provide an excellent cover for the action which the C-in-C thinks will provoke the Amis into an instant reaction – hopefully the destruction of the Monastery.'

'And the action, sir?' von Dodenburg asked.

'A raid in force behind the Ami lines, one which will make them howl with rage, which will demand a reaction from them on account of its sheer effrontery. Smiling Albert wants us to get the Amis by the tail and twist it until their eyes begin to pop. I don't know exactly how. It would depend upon the man on the spot. All I can say is that the C-in-C wants us to hit the enemy hard and hit him where it hurts the most – beneath the belt.' He looked at them challengingly. 'Gentlemen, I think I need to say no more. It is obvious why we have been honoured with the job, isn't it? Because the Regular Army regards Wotan as the only unit on this front capable of dirty work of that nature.' He smiled thinly. 'After all, we do have a certain reputation. Now may I ask for volunteers?'

Before Schwarz had clicked his heels together and stepped forward, von Dodenburg had raised his finger.

'I, Colonel,' he said coldly.

'Does that gesture mean you want to take a leak, von Dodenburg?' thc Vulture sneered.

The CO of the Wotan's Panzer Grenadiers ignored the insult.

'I shall take a half company,' he announced, as if the matter were already decided. 'Volunteers naturally.'

'What about me, Kuno?' Schwarz asked plaintively, his voice heavy with disappointment.

'No not you,' von Dodenburg said determinedly. He pointed a finger at the Creeper. 'I want him.'

'What me?' the Creeper quavered, his eyes full of sudden fear. 'But I'm only an observer here with Wotan.'

Von Dodenburg laughed humourlessly.

'Perhaps I need an observer, Lieutenant,' he said. 'You'll come along. I want to find out what you're made of.'

TWO

'Schulze – *now*;' von Dodenburg hissed urgently.

Schulze doubled forward, crouched low. The GI sentry never knew what hit him. Schulze reached up and pulled hard. The sentry's helmet slid backwards. With a deep grunt, Schulze grabbed the helmet thrusting his knee into the small of the Ami's back. Then he pulled with all his strength, Writhing desperately, his frantic fingers fighting to relieve the awful pressure, the young American was garrotted to death, as his chin strap bit deeper and deeper into his neck. Schulze lowered him gently.

'All clear,' he gasped and let the limp body slide down into the thick mud of the river bank. 'Come on.'

The volunteers slipped out of the bushes in which they had hidden themselves. Automatically, they began to strip. Now all was silent again save for the steady rumble of the heavies in the background and the urgent sound of their own breathing.

'Follow me,' snapped von Dodenburg, clad only in his underpants now. 'You, Kriecher, keep close to me.'

'But I've never done a river crossing at night before, Major,' the Creeper quavered, his body a fat amorphous blob in the faint pink glow of the Italian hamlet still burning to the Ami rear.

'Well, this is as good a time as any to learn,' replied von Dodenburg unsympathetically, slipping into the icy water, his gear wrapped in a groundsheet pushed in front of him.

'Come on. Heaven, arse and twine, man – the water won't bite you!'

Grumbling loudly, the Lieutenant hesitated until Schulze pretended to stumble against him. He fell with a startled yell full-length into the water. Despite himself he began to strike out for the opposite bank. The crossing of the Rapido after the retreating Amis was underway.

Just as the first wave of Wotan men reached the opposite

side, a flare shot into the air. For what seemed an age, it hung there bathing their naked bodies in its unreal, icy light. Then it sank to the ground with a soft hiss.

'Phew,' Schulze sighed with relief, 'I thought they had us there by the pisser!'

Von Dodenburg hid his own relief.

'You must be getting soft, Schulze. When Colonel Geier plans an operation, nothing like that can happen. He doesn't slip up. Perhaps it's that Ami holiday when they shoot off fireworks or something,' he added, slipping quickly into his wet clothes.

'Sure,' Schulze said sourly, following his example. 'Colonel Geier and his operations! If you ask me, this is a certain one-way ticket to the little fat-arsed boys with the wings on. A real old Ascension Day commando.'*

'Knock it off, Schulze,' snapped von Dodenburg, unslinging his Schmeisser and cocking it hastily. 'Let's move out.'

Yet, as his fifty-man patrol began to move cautiously towards the burning village a couple of kilometres away, he realized suddenly that by volunteering to lead the raid he had put himself exactly where the Vulture – if the latter knew by now his reaction to Schellenberg's offer – would want him to be: deep in the thickest shit. Hurriedly he dismissed the disquieting thought, and concentrated on moving in on the Italian village.

It was clear that the Amis were moving back in disorder. As they came into the village they could see the American tank destroyer abandoned in the middle of the road, one track stretched out behind it like a snapped limb. Beyond it was an abandoned truck, its windshield smashed into a glass spider's web. In their haste the Amis had even left the vehicle's engine running. Now the motor throbbed on uselessly, while the dead driver slumped over the wheel. Gently von Dodenburg pushed him to one side and turned off the engine.

'Young soldiers,' he said softly to Schulze, following close behind him, a sack of stick grenades around his neck. Schulze nodded.

* German Army slang for a hopeless mission (*transl.*).

'Easy meat, sir,' he agreed. 'What's the drill?'

Von Dodenburg grinned despite the unease nagging at him.

'The easiest, you big Hamburg clown. We'll go straight in, as if we belonged. *You*,' he swung round on the Creeper, who crouched, Schmeisser at the ready, as if the whole of the US Army were about to descend upon him personally at any moment. 'Kriecher, I mean you.'

With an effort of will the Creeper pulled himself together.

'Yes, Major?'

'I want you to cover us. If you hear anyone firing but ourselves, bring up the rest of the patrol through that side street there.'

'But how will I know the sound of the Ami weapons?' the strange SS officer asked miserably.

'Ami lead whistles "Yankee-Doodle-Dandy",' Schulze said in disgust and pushed by the cowering officer.

The village square, illuminated a blood-red by the flames of the burning houses, was packed with Amis. They were obviously beat, squatting on the kerbs, heads sunk between their knees, too worn and dejected to take one of the C-ration cans that a small group was heating in the flames. A big sergeant, who looked as if he hadn't shaved for days, was drinking out of a bottle of what looked like *grappa*, most of the fiery liquid running down his chin and soaking his shirt.

Keeping his eyes on them carefully, von Dodenburg used the traditional army hand signals to get his men into position; and like the trained killers they were, they glided noiselessly to left and right through the shadows into their designated spots.

'*Mary, Jesus, Joseph!*' one of the Tyrolean boys behind von Dodenburg whispered in awe. 'It's too easy . . . too easy, like shooting tame pigeons.',

'And you'll be a shitting dead pigeon in a minute if you don't hold your water,' Schulze cursed, reaching in his bag to pull out one of the stick grenades. 'Ready, sir!'

'Good.' Von Dodenburg raised his Schmeisser and tapped the long magazine to check if it were attached firmly. 'When I fire, let them have the first grenade – right in the centre of the square!'

Von Dodenburg raised the machine-pistol and swung it round looking for his first target. The thin barrel swung by two pale-faced boys dressed in long black raincoats, past an officer who had obviously torn at his badges of rank, as if in despair, and failed to pull them off, through a crowd of broad faces, innocent, von Dodenburg told himself, in a way that could be only American, and came to rest on the unshaven face of the drunken sergeant. For what seemed a long time von Dodenburg studied the face of the man he was going to kill. It was a good, tough face: the face of a man who had been let down and had become cynical, knowing that everyone could be bought some way or other. Suddenly he realized where he had seen that face before. With a sudden burst of rage, he pulled the trigger of his Schmeisser savagely.

The weapon chattered angrily. A stream of tracer shot through the air. The big NCO screamed, high and hysterical, like a woman. The bottle of *grappa* fell from his nerveless fingers to shatter on the cobbles. The face that had looked so like Wagner's became a pulp. What was left of his head struck the ground first.

The next instant the men posted all around the square opened up. Suddenly all was frenzied activity – screams, panic-stricken orders and counter-orders. The survivors of the 36th Division scattered desperately. But there was no shelter for them. A group of men who had been cooking over the flames pelted crazily for a lane. Schulze grunted and lobbed a grenade in their direction. It landed squarely in the centre of them. They went down screaming.

A hefty sergeant with shoulders bent forward like a footballer's, rushed at the unknown assailants, firing his tommy-gun from the hip. Von Dodenburg let him have a swift burst in the stomach. He careened round, still firing, spraying the sky with his slugs.

One of the boys in the long black raincoats tore towards the abandoned half-track. Von Dodenburg guessed instantly what he was intending. He pressed the trigger of his Schmeisser. Nothing happened.

'Great crap on the Christmas Tree!' he cursed bitterly and looked down. He had a stoppage.

'Get him!' he yelled desperately.

Zig-zagging crazily, the boy, his coat-tails flying wildly, dodged the stream of white tracer stitching an angry pattern around his heels. He faltered momentarily. He went on, but faltered again. Von Dodenburg could see the back material of the raincoat beginning to shine in the flames where the blood was pouring from the wound in his back. Then without any warning he pitched forward. Despite the vicious snap and crackle of the small arms fire, von Dodenburg could hear the slap of his face hitting the cobbles.

Now the panic-stricken Texans were beginning to raise their hands everywhere, some of them lifting their helmets like gentlemen passing a woman in a peacetime street.

'Cease fire,' von Dodenburg yelled urgently. 'Do you hear – save your ammunition, *cease fire*!'

Gradually the fire ebbed away, leaving behind no sound save the moans of the wounded and an echoing silence that seemed like eternity.

'Fifty dead, perhaps the same number wounded, sir,' Schulze reported, pushing back his helmet and wiping away the beads of sweat that had collected in the red puckered mark the helmet-liner made. 'Same number taken prisoner.'

'Thank you, Schulze,' the officer replied, fitting a new magazine to his Schmeisser, while the long line of prisoners against the wall eyed his movements in dumb apprehension.

The Creeper pushed his way through the chattering SS troopers, greedily spooning out chopped meat from the looted C ration cans.

'What are you going to do with them?' he asked eagerly, his nerve recovered now that the shooting was over.

'What do you suggest?' he answered, slinging the Schmeisser over his shoulder carelessly.

'Shoot them!' the Creeper rapped.

'Why?'

'Don't you see? If we slaughter the pigs,' he jerked a plump, well-manicured red thumb at the frightened prisoners, 'then we create the incident the Führer wants. It will cause an outrage among the Amis. I hear they worry about such trivialities.'

'Trivialities, eh' von Dodenburg echoed the word thoughtfully. Then his face hardened. 'Listen Kriecher, those are men – not trivialities. It is not necessary to shoot them; therefore they will not be shot. The night is still young and we have a lot to do. Do not fear, Kriecher, you will get your incident and the Führer's plan will be realized.'

'And the prisoners, sir,' Schulze butted in.

'Simple.' Von Dodenburg turned towards the wretched Amis. 'Listen,' he bellowed in halting English. 'I am to count to three. If you are not gone then – you are dead. You understand?' He raised his machine-pistol menacingly to emphasize his threat. 'That way. Now, get ready to run. One – two—'

Behind his back, the Creeper sneered:

'Why bother to save such rubbish? They are a burden to humanity. Look at them,' he nudged Schulze in the ribs, as the prisoners broke ranks and ran wildly down the lane leading out of the village, shouting fearfully and jostling each other in order to get out of the line of fire. 'A human rabble, not even worthy of a German bullet.'

That night the triumphant SS patrol ranged far and wide behind the American lines, burning, looting, destroying with impunity. The whole rear echelon was disorganized and apart from a few wild shots, no one attempted to stop them. A whole truck park went up in flames. A convoy of jeeps, speedily backing down a side road, ran into the looted Hawkins grenade daisy chain which they had spread across it. One after another they disappeared in vicious balls of flame. A group of tankers sleeping around their laager of Shermans were sent fleeing for their lives with a single burst of spandau so that the volunteers could destroy the six thirty-ton tanks at their leisure.

'Christ on a crutch,' young Bauer breathed, 'I can't believe it – it's just like being on manoeuvres back at Sennelager, with the old gentlemen of the Landwehr playing the enemy!'

'Don't take it for standard operation procedure, Bauer,' von Dodenburg warned. 'It isn't always as easy as this. This time we've caught them with their knickers down. But it won't always be like this, believe me.'

Just before dawn, as they emerged from a thick grove of

olive trees, the patrol almost bumped into the tented camp. Von Dodenburg held up his hand in warning. The SS men froze, while he surveyed the circle of bell-tents carefully. As far as he could see there were no guards and no other form of defence. The camp seemed to be asleep; there was no sound save an odd persistent thudding sound, which he could not immediately identify.

'Looks as if the Amis are getting in some sack time, sir,' Schulze suggested.

'Could be,' said von Dodenburg, surveying the lonely little encampment.

'But their security's pretty damn lousy even for the Amis.'

He made up his mind. In an hour or so, it would be light. This would be their last assignment; then they would have to make a rapid return to their own positions before the Amis were alerted and started to bring up the big battalions.

'All right, Bauer and you Kriecher, round to the right with your men. I'll take the left flank. And get the lead out of the men's arses – we're not going to spend more than fiften minutes here. You read me?'

With the Creeper nervously fumbling with his machine-pistol, the Bauer group disappeared round the side of the camp. Von Dodenburg spread his fingers on the crown of his helmet – the infantry signal for 'rally on em' – and with his men close on his heels, he doubled soundlessly for the nearest bell tent.

Silently they moved round the circle, scenting out potential danger. But there was no sound save the strange noise von Dodenburg had heard while they had still been in the olives. Now, as they came closer to it, von Dodenburg recognized it as that of someone digging, with every now and again the noise of a shovel being struck against the ground to free it of dirt. He halted a moment.

'Schulze, I'm going in alone. You cover me. But no firing unless it's absolutely necessary. We don't want to alarm the place until young Bauer has had a chance to get into position. Understand?'

Cautiously, his body crouched and tensed against the bullets that might come flying his way at any moment, von Dodenburg crept forward. Now he realized that the digging was accompanied by soft toneless humming. He took a deep breath and swung round the edge of the tent, finger gripped tautly over the Schmeisser's trigger.

A macabre scene met his eyes. In the hissing yellow light of a Coleman lantern, two middle-aged Negro soliders were digging a hole. Behind them lay four neat lines of khaki-clad corpses, rigid and motionless, staring sightlessly at the night sky, exactly as if they had died on parade. Von Dodenburg realized immediately who they were and what this place was – it was an Ami clearing station for the casualties of the abortive river crossing.

Waving a relaxed arm at Schulze and the rest to come up he stepped into the circle of flickering yellow light cast by the petroleum lantern resting on a ration box.

'Hands up!' he commanded.

The bigger of the two soldiers paused calmly in mid-stroke and raised his head with unhurried nonchalance. The other remained bent. He lifted his head slowly, however, his eyes filled with disapproval at this interruption of their work.

'I said – hands up!' von Dodenburg snapped as the rest of his men crowded in behind him and took in the strange scene, their tired eyes filled with awe. 'You are my prisoners.'

The bigger of the two took off his helmet liner and scratched his head with a dirty hand.

'Prisoners, you say? You a German, man?'

But before the young officer could answer the question the hysterical hiss of a Schmeisser machine-pistol had cut through the heavy pre-dawn silence.

As soon as they had burst dramatically into the first tent and found it full of nothing more dangerous than a semi-circle of wounded men lying on the floor, their arms attached to the life-giving drip-drip of the plasma bottles, snoring with the heavy, grating rasp of men under sedation, the Creeper had realized that this was it. As they entered the surgical tent, where the two surgeons were still operating in the blinding white circle of light cast by the hissing lanterns, their aprons stained up to the chest with blood, the Creeper knew definitely that he must seize this great opportunity to make the Führer's plan succeed.

'What the goddam hell are you doing nurse, to leave—'

The leading surgeon's cry of anger at the flap being opened behind his back died on his lips as he saw the two officers armed with machine-pistols standing there. Above the tight mask, his eyes flooded with fear. Then he pulled himself together. With a brisk nod, he indicated that the other surgeon, aided by an obviously severely frightened orderly, should continue their work on the leg of the man stretched out naked on the bloody table.

'What do you want?' he snapped in German.

'You speak German. Are you a Jew?' the Creeper asked.

'I asked you a question,' the surgeon retorted.

Behind him on the table, the other surgeon had begun to slice into the unconscious soldier's thigh with deft strokes. Blood began to gush out of the wounds. The frightened orderly tried to stem the bleeding, but his eyes were still on the intruders.

'You are in no position to ask questions,' the Creeper barked coldly. 'Here, I am the one who asks questions, do you understand?'

The head surgeon sighed wearily, his mask moving in and out as he did so.

'All right, then you are in charge. Now what do you want to know?'

Behind him the other surgeon had begun to cut through the thigh bone. The finely-toothed saw made a sickening grating sound as it bit into the bone. Bauer swallowed hard.

'Come on, Kriecher,' he said thickly, his mouth full of bile. 'Let's get out of here.' He dragged his eyes away from the blood-stained table. 'I'll puke up my ring soon if we don't.'

The Creeper did not take his eyes off the surgeon.

'All right, if you have no stomach for it, you'd better go now, Bauer. I'll handle this myself. Besides there will be worse to come.'

'What do you mean?' Bauer began.

But the words ended in a thick retch, as the other surgeon lifted up the nearly severed leg and holding it high with his free hand started to separate it completely from the bloody mess of the thigh. Bauer blundered out hurriedly, his hand pressed hard to his lips. Slowly the Creeper lifted his Schmeisser. The dark eyes watched him warily over the top of the face-mask. As Creeper clicked off the safety-catch, that wariness grew into fear.

'What do you think you're going to do, man?' the American cried.

At the table the other surgeon had finished. He allowed the severed leg to fall on to the bloodied floor.

'Pick it up,' he said automatically to the orderly.

The orderly did not react. He, like the senior surgeon, was staring as if mesmerized at the SS officer as he slowly swung the muzzle of his machine-pistol round to level on them.

'Will ya pick up the goddam leg, man. *For Chrissake!*' the other surgeon snarled angrily as he bent over the thigh.

Suddenly the orderly's mouth opened wide. His face crumpled. He screamed:

'Don't shoot – *please.*' He dropped to his knees, his hands held up in supplication. It was then that the Creeper fired. The blast of slugs at that short range threw the head surgeon bodily against the tent wall. He slumped down slowly, the blood streaming out of a dozen wounds across his riddled chest. The orderly's face disappeared in a welter of blood. The second surgeon slumped over the table, his head buried in the thick red mess of the unconscious man's stump. Wiping his mouth free of spittle with his left hand, the Creeper crossed the tent and held his machine-pistol against the unconscious man's head. He pulled the trigger. It was a short burst. But it was enough. The Ami's head shattered like that of a wax dummy. Blood and white fragments of bone shot everywere. Suddenly the whole side of the tent was dyed a bright red.

The Creeper hurried out, wiping his bloodied hand on the dead surgeon's gown with a grimace of disgust. A handful of SS men, who stood in a circle around the wretching Bauer, looked at him in alarm.

'What's the fireworks for?' someone cried.

'Hold your trap,' the Creeper snapped, completely in control now. 'You, you and you, fix bayonets and follow me – hurry now!'

'Fix bayonets – why?' someone queried.

'Don't ask questions, man,' the Creeper yelled. 'Your job is to obey orders. If you don't want to, you must take the consequences and believe me they won't be nice.'

Swiftly the SS men clamped their rifles between their knees and began to fix the bayonets to the end of the rifles. Bauer, supporting himself weakly against a tree, asked:

'What are you going to do, Kriecher?'

The Creeper didn't answer. Time was of the essence now. He had complete control and he was going to use it. There would be time for explanations afterwards.

'Follow me – at the double!'

Together with his squad, he burst into the first tent. It was filled with heavily sedated men. They bayoneted them easily, going from bed to bed with systematic cruelty. One man screamed, his spine arching his body in agony, before he slumped dead on the blood-stained cot. The rest died, not even aware that they had been slaughtered so brutally.

'Like sticking pigs,' a big rawboned South Tyrolean grunted as he placed his muddy boot on the chest of a dead American and pulled out his blood-stained bayonet, 'only this lot don't make so much noise as pigs do.'

The next tent's occupants were lightly wounded, and awake. They were desperately slashing at the rear canvas wall with surgical knives to cut a way out before it was too late. The Creeper fired a wild burst. A group of them went down still clawing at the canvas.

'No more firing,' the Creeper yelled above the screams. 'No more noise than necessary . . . use the cold steel.'

A sudden blood-lust had overcome the young SS men. They darted forward, springing over the rumpled beds to plunge their bayonets into the back of the terrified Americans. A big red-haired American loomed up in front of the Creeper. He ripped at the bandages covering the lower part of his face. They came away to reveal a shattered bloody mess below the mouth.

'Look, man,' he screamed in German, 'I'm shot – badly shot. You can't shoot me – my father came from Mannheim! Kurt Desch from Mannheim, Heidelberger Street thirty-six – everybody knew him in Mannheim. You can't—'

The words ended in a scream, as the Creeper smashed the

iron butt of his Schmeisser in his face. As he went down, the Creeper kicked him in the side of the head. His neck clicked back, spine broken. He was dead before he hit the floor.

Now they ran from tent to tent. The Creeper pelted into a tent, filled with lung cases.

'By the great whore of Buxtehude,' one of his panting men gasped, 'what a hell of a stench!'

'It's their lungs – they always stink like that when they've been hit in the pumps,' someone explained.

'We're doin 'em a favour then – to get them out of this shitty smell!' the first men yelled gleefully and reaching up, pulled down a long tube leading into one of the wounded Amis.

'What the tarnation is going on here?' a high-pitched female voice asked in English.

The Creeper swung round. A fat woman stood there, dressed in an olive-drab dress, the golden star of a major gleaming on the shoulder, her double chin trembling in righteous indignation.

'Will you look at that, you currant-crappers,' a soldier exclaimed in wonder, 'an Ami wench, right up here in the line. Do you think she does it for the soldiers.'

He grinned and thrust his thumb between his two fingers in the obscene gesture used by the troops.

'No,' someone else jeered. 'Ami wenches don't have one. You know what they say about 'em – whores in the kitchen and cooks in the bed!'

The others laughed uproariously. The American military nurse lunged at the man who had spoken. Before she reached him another man knocked off her gold-rimmed glasses. They fell to the floor and shattered. A laughing trooper pushed her. She fell over the metal side of a cot and sat down suddenly, her skirt riding up to reveal black pubic hair.

'Wow,' the laughing trooper who had pushed her over, breathed in mock wonder. 'Look at that! She's got one after all.' He made a play of fumbling with his flies with his free hand, looking at the Creeper. 'Shall I slip her a link, Lieutenant? A little fly one – something for her to remember us by!'

The Creeper's pudgy face flushed unpleasantly:

'No, we have no time for that kind of piggery. Let her stay alive. We need a witness to tell them what happened to her. But strip her. They tell me that the Amis are very moral in such things.'

Half a dozen laughing troopers dragged the woman up from the bed. She fought and scratched crazily as she sensed what they were going to do, but she was helpless in their hands. In an instant she was naked: narrow shoulders, great dangling breasts hanging over a pale scarred belly, her body shivering with cold and terror.

But the Creeper had no eyes for the naked American nurse. His mind was full of his scheme to ensure that the Führer's brilliant plan succeeded.

'You – and you,' he bellowed at the two men next to him. 'Take those bottles,' he indicated the ether bottles in the cabinet at the end of the tented room.

While they carried out his order, he himself slung extra blankets on each bed, spreading them over the unconscious Americans.

'Now splash plenty of it over the blankets,' he yelled.

The two soldiers ran from bed to bed throwing the liquid everywhere. As the tent filled with the heavy suffocating fumes, an Ami, who was awake and had tried to scream, heaved and twisted, attempting vainly to free his body from the stifling horror of the blankets.

'All right, outside everybody!' the Creeper cried, reaching in his pocket for his lighter.

'Oh my God!' the nurse screamed, her hands flying from a pathetic attempt to hide her sex, to cover her face in terror. 'You can't – you can't be that cruel!'

A young soldier punched her in the face. The nose shattered and blood shot everywhere. They kicked her outside, their muddy boots leaving dirty marks on her pale flesh.

The Creeper waited till they were clear. On the bed, the Ami tossed and turned, desperately trying to free himself, a strange bubbling sound escaping from his lips all the while. The Creeper backed to the flap and tossed the burning lighter onto the nearest ether-soaked blanket.

As he backed out, there was a muffled explosion. Flames ran up the sides of the tent, greedily eating up the canvas. The troopers scattered hastily, pushing the naked, sobbing nurse in front of them. The flames leapt higher and higher. Suddenly the man who had tried to escape appeared at the door of the tent. Tubes hung from him everywhere as he stood there blinded, the flames licking at his lower body.

'Help . . . help me!' he bubbled.

Behind the Creeper the nurse screamed and fell into the mud, as the wounded man staggered forward, his burning arms held upright in the shape of a cross. He didn't get far. He stumbled blindly over a crate and fell full length, a blazing torch for an instant, his head a blue flickering puddle of fire. The next moment he disappeared as the remaining bottles of ether inside the tent exploded. When the explosion had died away, he and the tent had vanished.

'My holy Christ, Kriecher!' von Dodenburg thundered, pushing back the crowd of SS men staring at the woman sobbing in the mud, her breasts smeared in blood, 'what's been going on here?'

The Creeper turned and faced him insolently. He waved a pudgy hand at the bullet-holed tents. 'It's obvious, isn't it, Major. Now the Führer has got his incident!'

Beside himself with rage, von Dodenburg laid Kriecher flat in the mud and brought up his Schmeisser.

'My God, Kriecher,' he cried thickly, 'they were wounded men!'

But just as von Dodenburg's forefinger started to squeeze the trigger, there was the faint but definite squeaky rattle of rusty tank tracks to the south. Von Dodenburg hesitated. He cocked his ear to the wind. They were definitely tracked vehicles; and there were no German tanks on this side of the River Rapido. He let the gun drop.

'You're a lucky swine, Kriecher.' He nodded to Schulze: 'Get the miserable bastard up out of the mud, will you?'

Schulze hurried forward and put his arms round the Lieutenant. As he did so, his fingers slipped into Kriecher's top left hand pocket.

'There you are sir,' he said dutifully, as he extracted the Creeper's notebook and slipped it inside his sleeve.

Von Dodenburg slipped off his long camouflage cape and drew it over the naked nurse sobbing brokenly in the mud.

'Here, place this on,' he whispered in his awkward English. Then he turned to the others:

'All right,' he said wearily, 'move it, men. Let's get our arses back across the river before the Ami armour gets here.'

He took one last glance at the ruined camp, full of slaughtered men, silent now save for the persistent sobbing of the nurse and the dying crackle of flames.

'I guess we've done what we came here to do.'

'You ain't shitting, sir!' Schulze said glumly, staring at the charred corpse still smoking at their feet. 'You ain't shitting . . .'

As the sun came up behind Cassino an angry blood-red, and the first enraged Ami barrage started to slam into the position at the top of Peak 555, the Wotan volunteers slipped across the Rapido again and commenced their weary progress up into the hills. The die was cast.

THREE

But nothing happened. Despite the massacre of the US clearing station, the Americans were apparently not prepared to retaliate. Indeed after a couple of days, the infuriated Ami bombardment of the Wotan positions on the peak died down completely; and the front settled into a strange brooding stalemate, with the fighting limited to sporadic patrol activity during the night.

At his headquarters in Rome, Kesselring questioned his staff every morning, half expecting that the Monastery had been attacked, half hoping it hadn't.

And morning after morning the same reply came back:

'Nothing new on the Cassino front, Field Marshal.'

The great Monastery, founded by St Benedict himself, had been saved for another day.

But if the Field Marshal, devout Catholic that he was, experienced a certain relief every time he learned that the Monastery was still intact, his master grew increasingly angry. Twice in the first week of February, 1944, he was called urgently to the telephone to hear that well-known voice demand:

'In heaven's name, Kesselring – how much longer must I wait?'

And all that an embarrassed Kesselring could reply was:

'Soon, my Führer, I promise you . . . Soon!'

On the Peak the officers of Wotan, who knew what had happened at the American hospital, were also puzzled. They spent hours searching the valley with their binoculars for some clue to the Ami intention, but they could discover nothing. As the Vulture remarked more than once:

'It almost looks, gentlemen, as if our American friends have packed their suitcases and returned to the land of unlimited possibilities, what?'

Life on the peak settled down into the dreary routine of

garrison duty, with inspections, regulation pre-dawn stand-tos and incessant weapon-cleaning. For von Dodenburg the lack of activity was a boon. It gave him time to think things out, steeled his resolve to do what he knew he had to do. But he realized now that there was more to do than just getting rid of the Vulture. He must ensure that the Wotan Battle Group did not fall into the wrong hands. There must be no more Geiers in charge of the Third Reich's elite formation. When the Vulture was dead, Wotan had to be his. There was no other alternative. But how was he to do it? How was he to kill the Vulture and still retain control of the Battle Group?

It was a problem that he had still not solved when the great clouds of dust, that seemed to spring up from nowhere on the white roads leading into the Liri, indicated that trouble was definitely brewing. The Vulture, alarmed by the outposts, lowered his binoculars and commented:

'Well, gentlemen, it looks as if we are receiving new guests. If I am not mistaken, our friends from that Empire upon which the sun never sets, are arriving down there. I suggest we set about ensuring that they receive a warm welcome. Gentlemen, *the Tommies are here*!'

But Colonel Geier was not altogether right. The troops who were flooding the valley below, relieving the beaten Americans of the US Second Corps, were not entirely British; they were General Freyberg's New Zealanders, and the tough New Zealander who had won the Victoria Cross in the First War, was not too happy with the situation. He kept glancing at the grim stone block which dominated the whole valley and his big tough jaw jutted out angrily as if he would ram it at the damned place at any minute.

Just before they parted that morning, General Gruenther* said a little wanly:

'Well, Freyberg, what do you think the chances are?'

The New Zealander hesitated a moment. He had never worked with the Yanks before; he did not know how they would take his legendary blunt honesty. He decided to risk it.

'Not more than fifty-fifty, General,' he growled. 'It's that

* Gen. Clark's Chief-of-Staff (*transl.*).

damn monastery up there. Gives me the creeps. It's like having someone watching you all the time even when you think you're in the privacy of your own thunderbox!'

Gruenther knew what the New Zealander meant. The place dominated the whole front. Perhaps the failure of the 36th on the Rapido was due to that too. Now, with the massacre of their rear elements by the Krauts, the survivors were in open rebellion. That very morning, the CIC had reported that a secret meeting of the 36th's junior officers had decided that they had been squandered unreasonably on the Rapido and they were proposing to raise the matter before Congress after the war. Morale was low enough in the Fifth Army without these new arrivals adding their own doubts to it.

'Oh, it isn't as bad as that, General,' he said. 'Our Intelligence, reports that the Krauts are not using the place for observation purposes.'

'Bugger Intelligence!' Freyberg answered crudely. 'I want the place taken out by air.'

Gruenther looked at him aghast.

'But you can't mean that, General?'

'I can and do. The place was converted into a fortress in the nineteenth century. The walls are a hundred and fifty feet high, of solid masonry and at least ten feet thick at the base. To cut a long story short, Monte Cassino is as powerful as any modern fortress and we've got to take it out by modern means.'

'But General—' Gruenther spluttered.

'No buts, General,' Freyberg interrupted brusquely. 'Whether the damn place is occupied by the Jerries or not at the moment is immaterial to me. They'll use it in the end, believe you me. Now General Gruenther,' he lowered his voice confidentially, 'this is what we're going to do.'

'Hot shit, Gruenther!' Clark cursed, 'that darn limey must be out of his mind! Do you realize what he wants me to authorize – our planes dropping blockbuster bombs on the goddam place! Can't you just hear the papers screaming in Boston? Goddamit Gruenther, those Catholics'd have the hide off me. And you can just imagine what the Pope's reaction would be.' He sighed wearily. 'Why is it everybody tries to sabotage me? What have

I done to deserve generals like this? I try my goddam best, and all I get is lousy goldbrickers.' Gruenther remained silent. He knew Clark, his moods of self-pity did not last long. Clark raised his head.

'What do you think, Gruenther?' he asked finally.

'Well, sir, the Second Corps has had the heart knocked out of it on the Cassino front. As you know, every time they formed up for an attack, the Krauts knew they were coming. 'Why?' He shrugged slightly. 'Because the Kraut observers in that damned monastery could see them coming. Okay, so now the limeys are going to have a crack and again the Monastery'll be signalling they're coming. In essence, sir, if you take it out, you'll have the Pope on your back; if you don't, you'll have Winnie Churchill breathing fire down on you. And I know which one of them is the worse.'

Three hours later the order went out from Clark's Fifth Army Headquarters to the United States Army Air Corps in Italy. It was brutally simple: *Destroy the Abbey of Monte Cassino.*

The gleaming silver planes came in at fifteen thousand feet, their white vapour trails sketching straight lines on the harsh winter-blue wash of the sky. They came on in perfect formation. Here and there a black puffball exploded about them. Down below in the Abbey, on this February morning, the Abbot knelt in front of the little Madonna of De Matteis and began to croak the words, 'Beseech Christ on our behalf', as the first bomb came thundering down. The great walls shuddered visibly. The dust of centuries was dislodged from the cracks. Another bomb fell and another, their thunder reverberating along the vast stone passages of the ancient pile so that they seemed no longer a series of individual explosions but one huge cataclysmic roar.

The monks, who had spent their lives hidden from the world in this mountain-top oasis of tranquillity, huddled together in terror. The wrinkled old Abbot commenced giving them absolution. Through the narrow windows the frightened monks, huddled in the corner, could see the blinding yellow flashes as treasure after treasure was destroyed, while the thunder of the explosions rolled back and forth down the vaulted corridors.

A servant stumbled in, his face contorted with shock. He was gesticulating wildly, but uttering no sound. His hands moved back and forth in a language none of the ashen-faced monks could understand. He was trying to tell them that the cathedral had just gone.

The four-engined Flying Forts had gone now. They had pounded the ancient monastery for four hours. Its roof was beginning to look jagged and uneven and here and there a window seemed unnaturally enlarged. But the place was still standing. Now it was the turn of the mediums; two-engined Mitchell bombers.

They came in at three hundred miles an hour – twelve of them in a tight aggressive formation. Watching them on Peak 555, von Dodenburg saw how their leader dipped his wings suddenly. It was the signal to attack. They roared in, the thin winter sun sparkling on their silver wings. Here and there the flak attempted to ward them off. But their speed was too great and they were too low for the 88s. Zooming through the cottony smoke, they came in for the kill.

Von Dodenburg started. Bright red flame spurted up at a dozen points as though a giant were striking matches against the mountainside. Almost instantly it was followed by a huge pillar of thick black smoke which rose straight upwards into the windstill blue sky until it was well over two hundred metres high.

'Oh, my aching arse,' Schulze breathed in awe, 'those blacks* are certainly getting a belting this day!'

Slowly the smoke started to clear, moving gradually so that what lay behind it appeared to shift and sway in sinister arabesques. At last the Monastery became visible again. Von Dodenburg whistled softly. Its whole outline had changed. The west wall had gone completely. The rest was in ruins. The Führer had his 'incident'.

Schulze got to his feet and stared at the ruin for a moment or two. A solitary green flare soared into the sky at the base of the Peak. For one long moment it hung there, bathing the slope in a

* Contemptuous SS name for a Catholic priest (*transl.*).

sickly light. Then it fell. As it did so, the slow heavy chatter of a Tommy bren began. Out of the rocks little brown figures in pudding-bowl helmets started to move forward cautiously, rifles held across their chests as they picked their way through the boulders.

'*An attack!*' young Bauer gasped and reached for his whistle to sound the alarm.

'Even as he did so, the first spandau hissed into action. Men pelted crazily to their foxholes. Von Dodenburg looked at Schulze grimly, his pale-face set.

'Well, you rogue, this is it.' He reached out his hand. 'Happy landings, Schulze!'

Schulze took his with genuine affection.

'And to you, sir! Mind you don't put your turnip up when you should be putting it down.'

Von Dodenburg swung round, crouched low and doubled madly for the sandbagged command post. Just as he reached it the full weight of the Tommy's creeping barrage hit the top of the mountain. The second battle for Cassino had commenced.

FOUR

The whole Liri Valley quaked with the roar. From end to end the angry red lights blinked like enormous blast furnaces. The whole weight of the New Zealanders' artillery smacked into action. With a hoarse scream, four hundred shells ripped through the sky over the advancing Indians' heads and crashed into the side of Peak 555. In an instant it had disappeared in a choking grey-yellow fog of acrid smoke and dust.

The men of Wotan huddled at the bottom of their bunkers, as the whole mountainside swayed and heaved like a ship at sea. Foxholes collapsed. Bleeding, screaming men fought the soil, scratching at it hysterically before they were choked to death. Behind the Twin Tits Command Post, the signallers' bunker received a direct hit. In an instant the trench had become a mess of dead and dying men, drowning in their own blood. Lieutenant Bauer, intent on setting an example to his new command by standing upright on the edge of his foxhole, as they had taught him to do at the cadet school of Bad Toelz, had his legs torn off. He bled to death, watching his severed legs with numbed curiosity and wondering if Sauerbruch might be able to sew them on again, while the blood poured out of his shattered stumps. The barrage stopped as startlingly as it had started. Its boom reverberated to and fro among the circle of hills and gradually died away. The men cowering at the bottom of the foxholes did not move until the wounded's faint cries of 'stretcher-bearer' alerted them to the danger. Hastily brushing off the dirt and rubble, they raised their heads. Bauer's machine gunner pushed his officer's mutilated body over the edge of the peak. It began to roll towards the enemy who were now only a hundred metres away.

Von Dodenburg sprang to the top of his CP. The mountainside was brown with the figures of Freyberg's turbaned 4th Indian Division. Sikhs, he told himself hurriedly, and blew a shrill blast on his whistle.

'*Now!*' he bellowed frantically and fired a wild burst at the Tommies.

The next instant he ducked as an Indian threw a grenade. It exploded over his shoulder, sending rock splinters and steel flying everywhere. Something slapped against his steel map case. It stung like hell. But he had no time to check if he had been wounded. The enemy were almost upon them now.

Bending double he ran towards his firing line. A dark-eyed face started up from somewhere. A heavy body crashed into him and he saw the man's bayonet fall to the rock. Automatically he fired a burst into the Indian. He went down on to one knee, his dark face contorted with pain and then leaped up again. He was too close for von Dodenburg to fire again. He aimed a kick at the man's groin. Like an eel he twisted to the right and avoided the kick. He grabbed von Dodenburg's neck. Von Dodenburg dropped his machine-pistol as the thin fingers dug deeply into his flesh. Suddenly he realized the man was some kind of unarmed combat expert. Twist and turn as he might, the Indian held on, blood pouring from his multiple wounds and soaking the German's tunic. Frantic with fear and lack of oxygen as he began to lose consciousness, von Dodenburg told himself that he was going to die. Then far away a well-known voice yelled:

'Get those shitty black hands off my officer!'

It was Schulze. The Reeperbahn equalizer crashed into the back of the Indian's neck. His spine arched and the grip slackened. Von Dodenburg stood there swaying, gasping for breath. The Indian dropped to the ground, his body quivering. Schulze ground his nailed heel into his face. Together they ran on.

The Indians were everywhere among their positions now. Schulze pulled out the china grenade ring and lobbed the bomb into the second wave. A second later he had waded into the confused mess of gasping men struggling back and forth on the crumbling edges of the foxholes. Von Dodenburg doubled past them leaving Schulze to do the best he could. Frantically he pushed aside the dead spandau gunner slumped over his weapon, and swung it round to face the second wave. The gun leaped to life under his hands.

The Indians of the second wave ran into a wall of lead. At

that distance von Dodenburg could not miss. Most of them lay where they fell in the scuffed, bloody dust. Others tried frantically to fight their way out of range. Von Dodenburg, crouched over the spandau, did not give them a chance. Riddled with bullets they dropped on to the grotesquely stacked bodies of their dead and dying comrades.

Behind him the first wave had been dealt with. The survivors of the Wotan perimeter doubled forward, panting asthmatically. They flopped into the dust and took up their firing positions, just as the third wave of Tommies came in.

This time the faces under the pudding-shaped helmets were white. Freyberg was sending in the British infantry component of his 4th Indian Division. But they died as easily and as swiftly as had his Sikhs and Rajputanas. Von Dodenburg's spandau burst into its high-pitched song of death once again. The tracer stitched a long line of red and white lead along the line of the advancing Sussex. The British, advancing in perfect formation as if on parade, went down in droves. But still they came.

'That Tommy's mine!' Schulze cried above the chatter of the spandau. He pulled the string out of a potato masher. It sailed slowly through the air. If the British infantry saw it, they did not let it disturb their measured pace. It exploded beneath the tall officer.

The death of the CO was enough for the Sussex. Still firing, trying to hold their shattered formation, they began to back down the slope the way they had come, firing at regular intervals. But there was no joy in von Dodenburg's heart as the Tommies started to clear the hillside. For as the firing started to die down, he could hear the rusty rumble of tracks and the grind of powerful engines trying to ascend the khaki-littered slope in low gear. And he knew what that meant: the British were bringing up tanks.

'Well?' the Vulture snapped, as von Dodenburg stumbled into the Twin Tits' CP, his tunic covered with blood, his face black with powder burns.

'We held them,' the Panzer Grenadier CO gasped. 'But only just.'

'A cup of nigger's sweat – I've laced it with grappa,' Metzger thrust a cup of steaming black coffee in front of him.

Von Dodenburg knocked it aside.

'I haven't got time for your coffee, Metzger. The Tommies are bringing up tanks!'

The Vulture's monocle popped out of his eye.

'But they can't get tanks up that slope!' he protested.

'They always say God is on the side of the big battalions, sir. Perhaps they prayed. At all events, we can hear tanks down there on our sector of the perimeter.'

'All right, what do you suggest, von Dodenburg? The recoilless rifles? I can let you have one.'

'One!' von Dodenburg exploded.

'Yes. Your position is very exposed. If you're overrun, I can't afford to lose the little heavy stuff I've got.' The Vulture smiled cynically.

'You mean—'

'I mean,' the Vulture cut him short, 'you have picked the wrong side, my dear chap.'

The vehicles von Dodenburg had heard were not in fact tanks. They were something worse: little tracked vehicles, which he knew the Tommies called Wasps*, armed with strange snub-nosed cannon attached to trailer tanks which bumped up and down behind them. Schulze, crouched with von Dodenburg and the Creeper behind the recoilless rifle, groaned out loud as the Wasps ground closer and closer, their infantry tightly packed behind their cover.

'Oh my sodding aunt – flame-throwers!'

Von Dodenburg gulped with fear. A vision of his childhood flashed through his brain: Colonel-General Hammerschmitt unwrapping the black bandage he always wore around his head to reveal a bald head, yellow and wrinkled like that of some Egyptian mummy, with two dark holes where the ears should have been.

'A flame-thrower – he was caught by a Frog flame-thrower at Verdun in sixteen, that's all my boy.'

His father had comforted him when he had run screaming to

* A modified bren-gun carrier (*transl.*).

blab out what he had seen in the bedroom. But he hadn't slept well for many a month after that. Now he was to face up to that most terrible weapon himself.

A slug from one of the Sussex's snipers flattened itself on the rock next to him. The Creeper yelped with fear. Von Dodenburg ignored him.

'Listen, Schulze,' he rapped, not taking his eyes off the slow-moving Wasps for one instant. 'We've only one chance. We've got to hit the bastards quick – one, two, three. You've got to load and re-load damn smartish.'

'Don't worry about me, sir,' Schulze said, licking his dry lips. 'You concentrate on knocking the sods out. I'll go at the loading like a squaddie at his missus after four months in Russia.'

'Good.' Von Dodenburg jabbed his elbow in to the Creeper's ribs viciously. 'And you – let's have those shells coming right quick.

The leading Wasp was less than two hundred metres away now, grinding up the steep slope with difficulty, its following infantry tense and ready for the killing. Von Dodenburg swallowed hard. The little Tommy vehicle was still out of range. He kicked the tripod to check whether it was set firmly and then crouching behind the strange weapon again began to follow the Wasp's slow approach.

Now the snipers, hidden in the rocks all around, opened up knowing that they must keep the Germans' heads down and cover the carriers' advance. Slugs struck and whined off the rocks. Creeper's face blanched. The Wasp's gunner pressed the trigger. There was a hushed intake of air. A forked tongue of oil-flecked flame shot out a good hundred metres. The dust shrank in its path. But it was still short of their positions. Before their horrified eyes, the boulders twenty metres away turned a dull glowing purple. The heat was horrific. They felt their breath dragged forcibly from their lungs.

Von Dodenburg wiped the sweat from his brow and felt his cheeks glow with the heat. Again the long tongue of flame licked out at them greedily. They ducked hurriedly. Von Dodenburg felt his tunic begin to singe. There was a smell of burning cloth and hair. He gasped for breath like a fish in its death throes. It was now or never. He peered through the sight. The Wasp rattled into the centre of the crossed lines. He could see the white blob of the driver now through the slit in the armour. Behind it he glimpsed the helmets of the infantry. He pulled the firing bar.

There was a dry crack. A wave of acrid fumes slapped him in the face. Automatically he opened his mouth to prevent his eardrums from shattering.

'*Now!*' he yelled above the roar of the explosion.

Schulze slammed home another shell into the gaping breech. Metal struck metal with a hollow boom. The Wasp came to an abrupt halt, a bright hole in its side. White smoke started to pour from its engine.

'*You hit it, sir!*' Schulze shouted exuberantly, as the crew bailed out.

But von Dodenburg had no time to enjoy his triumph. The remaining two Wasps were still coming on past the stricken flame-thrower. The first one came parallel with it and fired immediately. The flame engulfed a bunker to their right. Two young troopers ran out, screaming frantically. Before they had gone five metres, they had been consumed by the greedy flames. They dropped slowly to the ground, charred black and shrunken already to the size of pigmies.

Behind von Dodenburg, the Creeper retched violently. His bile rose and he spewed over the back of the Major's tunic. In that same instant, von Dodenburg pulled the firing bar again. The gun crashed into action. The shell hit the Wasp squarely in the bogies. The stricken Wasp swung round, smashed to one side by the force of the blow. The gunner slumped dead over his weapon. His hand still on the trigger. A fatal oversight.

The terrible weapon fired of its own accord. The flame engulfed the Sussexs following it. In an instant all was chaos. The dead gunner kept the gun flaming, wreathing them in its fiery blast. One by one they dropped, screaming frantically, charred skeletons.

It was too much for the remaining Wasp. It swung round crazily on its axis. With a crash of gears, the maddened driver shot forward, cutting a great swathe through the following infantry, scattering them on both sides, leaving a crushed pulp of dead men behind as it scurried down the steep hillside. The next instant the terrified survivors fled, and the second Wasp's flame-thrower finally fell silent.

Von Dodenburg sat down abruptly in front of a sobbing Creeper.

'Let them go, Schulze,' he breathed and pushed back his helmet from his blackened, sweat-lathered face, as the big Hamburger raised his Schmeisser. 'The poor bastards have had enough.' He gulped in a deep breath of the cold air gratefully. 'Don't worry, they'll be back . . .'

FIVE

They were. Time and time again. Sussexs and Sikhs. Rajputs and Royals. One day their attackers would be black men; another white men. Sometimes they seemed neither one colour nor another. The New Zealand Maoris came rushing up the hill. Burly men, who looked a little too heavy to be good infantry in von Dodenburg's opinion. They got to within fifty metres of the Panzer Grenadiers' positions – all shining Polynesian faces and big white teeth. They melted away in front of the massed machine-guns.

Once their attackers were yellow, and they came by night: the stocky little mountaineers of the 1st/2nd Gurkhas. Unlike the others they tried to outflank the position, climbing up and beyond the perimeter and coming down near to the Twin Tits just before dawn. But the Vulture had anticipated even that approach, although Kesselring, who knew something about mountain warfare himself, had told him it was impossible. He had strewn the area with their home-made 'deballockers', as Schulze called the primitive anti-personnel devices: a bullet inserted in a little container, which sent the bullet flying upwards at groin-height if anyone stepped on it.

'You might live after you step on one,' Schulze was wont to comment about them. 'But you ain't going to be much good in the hay afterwards!'

The Ghurkas' leading platoons came swinging confidently from the height right into the minefield, their kukris held at the ready. Before they had a chance to use their deadly curved knives there was a series of staccato explosions. The little men howled and clutched at their shattered crotches, letting their kukris fall. A moment later the flares hissed into the night, casting their ruddy unreal light on the terrible sight below. The spandaus opened up. The Gurkhas' Colonel went down with a slug in the base of his stomach. He called the next wave to attack. They ran over the tormented bodies of their injured comrades. But they could not break through the line of spandaus. By dawn there was little left of the 1st/2nd Gurkha Rifles.

Freyberg sent in the Fortresses. They came at fifteen thousand feet. To von Dodenburg crouched at the bottom of his command bunker the four-engined bombers, pressing on steadily towards their position, looked beautiful and arrogant. When their bombs came whistling down with their messages of death, it seemed to him that at that height the war must have appeared very remote to those flying supermen, busy with their dials and buttons.

But the bombs did not dislodge the tenacious defenders of Peak 555, although they were taking serious casualties. Now most of the bunkers dug in around the Twin Tits were filled to overflowing, and the Battle Group's two surgeons worked night and day trying to save the wounded. But as February gave way to March time began to run out. The Chief Surgeon who looked more like a butcher in his blood-stained rubber overall and gumboots than a doctor, told von Dodenburg when he came to visit some of his own wounded Panzer Grenadiers:

'Nowadays, von Dodenburg, we have no time for the difficulties occasioned by complicated wounds. Our rule now is – head or belly shot, curtains.'

He made the gesture of shooting a hypodermic into a man's arm.

The pile of dead, stacked there like logs of wood, began to grow behind the Twin Tits. And as the first of the spring sun began to warm the shell-pocked landscape, the flies appeared. They feasted, while the shocked, ashen-faced Grenadiers defending the height starved. Big flies that looked like black Italian grapes on wings: flies on the dead; flies on the wounded; flies on the faeces that lay everywhere among the shattered rock. For them there was food enough and no amount of gluttony could satiate them as they buzzed lazily over the dead and dying strewn over the height, enjoying the warming rays of the sun and dimming the sunlight when they rose in one of their swarms.

The Grenadiers took to wearing crude masks and in quiet

periods they lit smoke pots, filled with the bloody rags torn off the dead, to ward them off. But the flies always came back. As an exhausted Schulze said vehemently, giving up his attempts to fight them off:

'If you ask me – the only shitting things which enjoy this war is those shitting turds of flies!'

One day the venerable Abbot of Monte Cassino was waylaid on the road to Rome by Goebbels' agents and forced into a series of broadcasts denouncing the 'Allies' barbaric bombing of one of Europe's foremost cultural treasures'. The same week the steam went out of Freyberg's attack on the Cassino front. As he told a worried Clark, 'going to give my chaps a ruddy breather, you know'.

But the 'ruddy breather' did not help the men of Wotan trapped on a square kilometer of shell-pitted mountain top. Now they were hemmed in on three sides, with the New Zealanders dug in further down the slope, their positions permanently covered by a thick brown fog of smoke. But at night when the heavies had stopped their barrage, Wotan's sentries could hear the enemy coughing or whispering softly together and they knew the New Zealanders were not much more than fifty metres away.

It was on one such night that the Vulture, his body filthy and unwashed, decided that he would sneak through their perimeter and crawl up the mountainside behind them to the stream which supplied them with their water, to wash off some of the last few days' grime.

It was a beautiful night, the sky above the peak silver with moonlight, with the faint breeze from the south warm and balmy. Down on the slope the New Zealand positions were silent and wreathed, as ever, in smoke from the pots they kept burning permanently in front of their trenches. The Vulture decided that he could confidently anticipate no trouble this pleasant spring night. All the same he warned the sentries where he was going and told them to be on the alert in case he ran into trouble. Then he set off alone up the sparkling, silver mountainside, his mind full, not only of his own situation, but of that of Germany in general.

So far Wotan had managed to hold back the Allied drive for Cassino; the door to Rome was still held, but only just. The bombing of the Monastery had shown to what lengths they would go in their drive north to Rome and then on to the Reich itself. Soon Schellenberg in Berlin would have to make his decision about Hitler. Then, he, Geier, would have to make his own decision. But could he rely on that young fool von Dodenburg to bring his devoted Panzer Grenadiers in on the side of the conspirators when the time came?

Ever since he had come back from Berlin, von Dodenburg had acted very strangely, seeming to avoid him; and in the heat of the battles of these last few weeks he had had no chance to question him. If he only knew what had gone on in Berlin when von Dodenburg had met Schellenberg! But he didn't. It had not been safe to contact Wagner since the offensive started. And that damn little spy Kriecher seemed to be everywhere, listening and making notes. One day, he promised himself, he'd put a bullet in the back of the pudgy, bespectacled Lieutenant.

Thus preoccupied, Colonel Geier, undressed save for his riding boots, stowed his monocle carefully in the pocket of his cavalry breeches and stepped gingerly into the little mountain stream. The water was icy-cold as he scooped up a handful to splash on his naked body, but it was good. He shivered with both pleasure and the cold, and began to wash the stink and grime of battle off his body. There was no sound save the persistent dry cough of a machine-gun far away.

Suddenly he froze. Something or someone was splashing down the stream toward the huge rock which blocked his vision. The splashing sounds came nearer. Then stopped. The Vulture tensed himself. Should he attempt to rush to the bank for his pistol? The other man, if he were armed, would be round the rock, shooting before he could make it. So that was out.

He could hear someone scooping up water, then a faint gasp of shock. It was a man all right and not some stray animal. Could it be one of his own men? Why didn't the damn fellow say something so that he could identify him? In the next instant the other person came round the bend, splashing the water with his bare feet. For a moment the Vulture thought he was facing some Italian woman. The hair was jet-black to the shoulders and the skin was a warm brown. But the absence of breasts and the prominent sexual organ told him that this was no woman. This was a man: a handsome young Sikh.

For what seemed an eternity, the two men stared at each other, bodies slightly hunched, breath coming in shallow gasps. The Vulture could see that the other man's mind was working like his own. If he yelled for help, he might alert his own sentries, but there was the danger that the Sikh had not ventured into this no-man's land alone; there could well be more of them somewhere in the rocks.

Suddenly the Sikh lunged forward, the water dripping from his naked body. The Vulture side-stepped and grabbed at his body. He missed, hands slipping off the wet skin. But the Sikh didn't. His strong arms encircled the German. With a grunt he pressed his own body against the Vulture's. Despite his fear, the Vulture felt a shiver of pleasure run through him.

The young Sikh was trying to force him into the deeper water. The Vulture guessed his intention at once. But the other man was as slippery as an eel. Every time Geier tried to knee him, he avoided the blow. Now he pressed his abdomen lightly to the Vulture's so that the latter could use his knee no longer.

In slow motion, they struggled back and forth in the waist-deep water, silent except for an occasional grunt. The Vulture hooked two fingers inside the Sikh's broad nostrils trying in vain to tear the flesh upwards and break the wrestler's hold. The Sikh wriggled his head loose and pressed his face close to the Vulture's cheek so that he could not attempt the same move again.

Viciously the Sikh reached up one hand, still retaining his hold on the Vulture with the other, and tried to jam his fingers into the German's eyes. With difficulty, because of the hold the Sikh had on him, the Vulture dodged the blow. Gasping frantically, he twisted to one side and grabbed at the Sikh's genitals. His fingers contacted the hot flesh. He squeezed hard. The Sikh screamed in agony. He broke his hold almost immediately. The Vulture swiftly caught his right arm. With a deft gesture, he forced it behind the Sikh's back and propelled him forward.

Geier drew a swift gasp of air. Before him the moonlight gleamed along the length of the boy's brown, muscular back. The next instant he forced the Sikh's face under the water. The Sikh's scream ended in a series of violent bubbles. Frantically he attempted to lash out with the heel of his right foot. The Vulture avoided the blow easily. His arms threshed the surface of the stream into a white fury and the Vulture forced his head deeper and deeper below the water. Still he held on. His boots gave him a firm grip on the pebbled bottom which the boy's wild struggles could not shake. Geier closed his eyes, the buttocks brushing his naked loins time and time again. The Sikh's struggles grew weaker. He gave a last, desperate twist just before he began to drown. Then he went limp.

Finally the Vulture opened his eyes, and released his grip. For a couple of seconds he could see nothing, save the white eddies of water caused by the Sikh's desperate struggles to break free. Then the body emerged on the surface a metre away. For a brief instant Geier gazed down at the Sikh's handsome young face; then slowly he bent and pressed his lips on the dead boy's.

It was much later that same night that the Vulture, still trembling with both fear and memory of that naked brown body, began the encoding of the message he would radio to Kesselring's Operations Officer to pass on to Schellenberg. As he did so, he tried to control the turmoil of his mind. The brief deadly contact with that unknown enemy had awakened the old desires in him. His imagination was flooded with half-forgotten memories of the beautiful young boys with powdered faces and pencilled, plucked eyebrows he used to meet furtively behind the Lehrter Station before the war; the warm olive skin of the young Italian officer who had been his so briefly last summer before the partisans had captured him and put him to death. Now all he wanted was to bury himself in the arms of some young man, forget the horror of the peak and everything that went with it. He had had enough of a war where he had to kill a man, who under other circumstances would have been able to give him so much pleasure. Forcing himself to concentrate, he spelled out the decisive message:

'WOTAN STILL HOLDING. NEXT OFFENSIVE WILL MEAN END. SUGGEST URGENTLY ARRANGE EVACUATION OF SELF AND KEY CADRE AT OPPORTUNE MOMENT *SOONEST*. WOTAN TO BE REFORMED IN GERMANY IN OUR SENSE BY CADRE. CADRE TO BE PICKED BY ME. EXPEDITE.

GEIER'.

But even as he wrote the Vulture could not stop his hand trembling. After four years of war, the Commander of Wotan, Nazi Germany's elite formation, the nerveless Colonel Geier had reached breaking point.

SIX

The New Zealanders attacked for the last time on the day that Schulze stole the Vulture's sole remaining pig. At least that was how von Dodenburg remembered the final offensive in the years to come.

It had been sunny for many days. Even the grim desolation of war could not destroy the beauty of the Italian countryside. Admittedly the slopes of Peak 555 bristled with the lacerated stumps of acacia and olive trees. But the Liri Valley below was soft and green again. No artillery bombardment on earth could have stopped the wild corn from growing, or the red poppies. And behind them on Monte Cassino, the honey-coloured ruin of the Monastery glowed pink and gold in the morning sunshine.

But on that particular morning, Schulze had no eyes for the beauty of the scene. His sights were set on food. As he had told the little group of Panzer Grenadiers under his command:

'I've had enough of that shitty 'Old Man' and giddiup soup! This morning when I got up, the first thing I did was to neigh and the second – to cock up my leg and piss!'

Now Schulze wandered morosely about the plateau, wondering where he might get some fresh meat on such a fine spring day. Everywhere the hard-pressed defenders were stripping off their tattered grey shirts, looking for lice, allowing the first warm rays of the sun to brown their emaciated bodies, or crouching over their home-made stoves (ration cans, half-filled with dirt, soaked with petrol and ignited) cooking their morning rations. He had just passed the HQ's latrine – a long pole stretched between two ration boxes over a lime-and-faeces filled pit – when he first smelled *real* meat cooking.

The Creeper and Captain Schwarz were perched on the latrine, discussing whether their Japanese allies could really be classed as 'honorary Aryans'. Schulze flung them a magnificent salute as he passed, his nose twitching as he tried to ascertain the direction from which the delectable odour was coming. Then he spotted it. The ex-butcher, Sergeant Metzger, was crouched to the right of the Twin Tits, cleaning his nails with a bayonet, the stump of an unlit cigar clamped between his gold front teeth. Trying to restrain his mounting excitement Schulze sauntered up to the big NCO, gave him a casual salute* and asked:

'What's on the menu for the Old Man, Metzger?'

'Stewed socks and toerag dumplings,' Metzger replied tight-lipped.

'Same as us,' Schulze said carefully. He made a show of sniffing the air. 'Though I did think that I could smell pork cooking somewhere or other.'

Metzger looked at him coolly.

'So-so.' He finished cleaning his fingernails and used the bayonet to poke at the gaps between his teeth. 'Your nose must be too close to your own arsehole – that's what you can smell.'

'Perhaps so, Metzger,' Schulze answered gloomily. 'Must be getting light-headed from the lack of fodder, eh? Though,' he hesitated, 'I could swear I smell meat roasting somewhere.'

He flashed a look around the area and spotted it: a thin blue haze rising from a pile of rocks some twenty metres away! The bastard of a butcher had hidden his stove over there. There was no denying the heat haze rippling in the thin rays of the morning sun.

'Notice you haven't got your last pig any more,' he said casually.

'Got his in the last shelling,' Metzger replied carelessly. 'Poor bastard – disappeared completely. Direct hit.'

'Oh, I see.' Schulze made a play of absorbing the information for a few moments. 'Well, I suppose I'd better go and take a crap while it's still quiet. Yesterday one of my heroes fell in the pit as soon as the Ami shelling started. Don't want that to happen to Mrs Schulze's little boy.'

'Couldn't happen to a nicer bloke,' Metzger commented, his eyes fixed on the rocks which hid the stove.

'Thanks, Metzger,' Schulze said as he strolled away aimlessly. 'I'll do the same for you some time.'

* In the SS, NCOs were saluted (*transl.*).

Moments later he was doubling up the slope beyond the stove and out of Metzger's sight. Silhouetted against the slanting rays of the morning sun from the east, he made a perfect target for any Tommy sniper. But his mind was set on cutlets. His plan was simple and it worked perfectly. Pulling out his last phosphorous grenade, he ripped the pin out with his teeth, balancing his machine-pistol with the other hand. The next minute he had lobbed it high over the rocks in Metzger's direction, white smoke already trailing from it. As it exploded with a crump on the other side and the thick fog started to shoot up, he fired a wild burst wih his Schmeisser and yelled:

'*Alarm . . . alarm . . . stand to, here come the Tommies!*'

Clasping his hand over his nose and keeping his mouth tightly shut, he slid down the rock into the smoke. For a moment or two he blundered blindly around in the fog while Metzger bolted for the safety of the Twin Tits. Then Schulze spotted the stove. Ignoring the leaping flames, he grabbed the big pot in which the cutlets were roasting. A second later he was running towards his own position, laughing till the tears ran down his face. The cutlets were his.

'My God, Schulze,' von Dodenburg said happily, munching the rather undercooked meat, grease dribbling down the blond stubble on his chin, 'you're a genius – an absolute genius.'

'Thank you, sir.'

'Yes,' von Dodenburg went on. 'You're the kind of chap, Schulze, who would very probably stumble over a case of champus – *French* champus – in the middle of the Sahara Desert.'

'I'd rather stumble over a piece of ass up here at the moment, sir, if you don't mind.' Schulze belched and threw his bone away. 'All that meat does something for the inner pigdog.' He wiped the grease off his lips. 'Puts lead in your pencil. Makes your mind start wandering to higher things – dames, dames with big lungs on them and minus their drawers.'

Von Dodenburg laughed. He wiped his greasy hands on the piece of rag he used to clean his Schmeisser.

'Wonder what they'll be eating at the Twin Tits this day?' he said reflectively, picking at a piece of meat which had lodged between his teeth.

'Giddiup soup, I shouldn't be surprised. One of the mules got hit yesterday night bringing up the ammo.'

Von Dodenburg leaned back and allowed the warming rays of the sun to play on his face.

'I'm afraid Lieutenant Kriecher will be in trouble again. The Colonel made him responsible for the mules' safety.' He grinned. 'Between you and me, he said that was all Kriecher was good for – one horse's arse to look after other horses' arses, were his words.'

Schulze shook his head.

'Don't think so, sir. The Creeper will be the last man to get into trouble, if you ask me.'

'What do you mean?'

'Do you remember the night of the patrol – when you pushed him down? Well, I helped him up and' – he hesitated – 'this sort of fell into my hand.' He reached into his tunic and pulled out the Creeper's notebook.

'Well?'

'It's the Creeper's notebook, sir. He's got us all in it in alphabetical order.'

'What do you mean – got us all in?'

'Let me show you, sir.' Schulze licked his dirty thumb and leafed quickly through the dog-eared pages. 'This is me – the Creeper's assessment of Mrs Schulze's boy.' He lowered his voice. ' "Schulze, holder of Knight's Cross. Ex-NCO. Demoted for some offence unknown to me. Confident of Major D" – that's you, sir . . . Now, here's the assessment. "Typical big-mouthed waterfront red from Hamburg. Stupid, insolent, does his utmost to undermine the loyal men and destroy their National Socialist fervour." ' He looked up at his CO. 'Now what do you say to that, sir?'

'Is there anything on me?'

'A bit, sir. Not much. Here we are. "Major von Dodenburg. Knight's Cross, German Cross in Gold, silver wound medal—" '

'Skip the details of the tin,' von Dodenburg interrupted. 'Let me have his assessment.'

' "Comes of a family of Prussian military aristocrats. Represents his class point-of-view, but a previous impressive record of National Socialist loyalty. Now undecided. To be watched." And that last bit is underlined in red ink, sir.' He looked up, worried. 'You and the Colonel are the only ones to have entries in red ink, by the way, sir.'

'And the Colonel's?'

'Only one word, sir.' Schulze hesitated, as if embarrassed.

'Well, spit it out!'

Schulze licked his dry lips.

'It's . . . well, it's traitor, sir. One word, underlined in red ink – traitor!'

Von Dodenburg broke the heavy silence. A few metres away the rest were squashing lice eggs between thumb and finger and counting their score.

'So, the Creeper's a Gestapo spy, you think, Schulze?'

'Looks like it, sir. He obviously isn't a combat officer – the four-eyed little bastard. Prince Albrecht Strasse sent him here to spy on us poor old stubble-hoppers. God knows why! We're not going to live long enough on this shitty hill to ever be brought to trial, though what the hell we're supposed to have done wrong, I'll never know.'

Von Dodenburg shook his head.

'It's the same everywhere, Schulze. There's something very wrong with the Homeland. I saw that when we were in Berlin. There are traitors everywhere – men who wear the same uniform as we do, but who no longer believe in what we believe.'

'Who does?' Schulze asked cynically.

'I do!' von Dodenburg said harshly, his face set and hard. I believe that we must win, because – if nothing else – there is no other alternative left open to us. If we lose, the Amis will have the eggs off us with a blunt razor-blade. Make no mistake Schulze, if we lose this war, it will be the end of the Germany we know. They'll reduce us to the level of a slave state, based on an agricultural economy, which will be allowed to produce enough food to prevent us from starving, but nothing more. As for people like ourselves – members of a formation such as the Wotan – we're for the high jump, a quick short walk at the end of a hangman's noose. We're hopelessly compromised in their eyes.'

'You mean the hospital?'

'Yes, and a half a dozen other similar incidents over these four years. We've fought a hard war, Schulze – a very hard war. If we lose it, we have to pay the price. We have to fight on, you see. It's as simple as that.'

Down in the valley the heavies were beginning to rumble again.

'But if you'll forgive me, sir,' Schulze said. 'The folks back home have had a noseful. They've had it up to here.' The big soldier drew a dirty forefinger under his nose. 'The bombs, the rationing, the killing – everything. But I don't have to tell you that, sir! As for us lot out here – the front swine – we don't like the war any better. We have to fight on because if we don't—' He broke off, making a trigger of his forefinger. 'That's the honest truth. That's the way it is in the Homeland and out here too. We've had it, sir.'

'We haven't, Schulze!' von Dodenburg retorted hotly. 'Besides, as I've already said, we have no alternative; we have to fight on.'

'But how, sir?'

'How?' the officer laughed mirthlessly. 'Simple. We have to rely on ourselves absolutely. Not another battalion. Not another regiment. *But on this one unit!* The Wotan will have to replace our homeland, our family, our organization. It must have our sole and absolute loyalty, then we might have a chance.' He leaned forward fervently, his fists clenched, his eyes hard and staring. 'Don't you see, Schulze? If we stick together, nothing can stop us. We might even inspire the whole army to new efforts. Remember the Führer started the whole movement with exactly seven men – seven men, mark you. And we're still a good three hundred or more left standing.' He paused for breath.

'And the CO?'

'You read the Creeper's assessment, didn't you?' von Dodenburg's voice was cold.

'Then it's true?'

'Yes.'

'So what are you going to do with him, sir?'

'There is only one thing I can do, Schulze.' Von Dodenburg tapped his pistol holster.

Down below in the Allied positions, preparations were being made for the last offensive to kill the survivors of Wotan. Maps and orders were checked for the last time. Fitters and drivers squirmed from under their vehicles, confident that they were in perfect condition. Stores and ammunition were stowed in the backs of the trucks and tanks. Officers and NCOs held their final conferences and briefings.

Those with nothing to do now slept in the sunshine, but these were the old sweats. The new men – and there were many of them – sat around and tried to hide their fear and uncertainty by telling dirty jokes. Some wrote letters beginning with the traditional line:

'If you don't hear from me for a little while, don't worry . . .'

A few prayed. By the late afternoon everything had been done. The guns had ceased firing, saving their ammunition for the great bombardment which would herald the advance. A strange silence descended upon the Cassino front: a silence heavy with tension and menace. The German guns fell silent too.

As the hours ticked by to H-hour the silence grew more oppressive. An artillery commander, thinking that the Germans might become suspicious at the lack of fire, ordered a few shells to be aimed at the enemy. The waiting infantry breathed a sigh of relief as the 25-pounders thundered into action. Silence at the front was something sinister. The situation now seemed normal again. They relaxed.

The sun went down, sliding blood-red behind the mountains which barred the way to Rome. A little later the stars came out, bathing the land in silver. The commanders began to glance more frequently at the luminous dials of their watches.

At eleven o'clock precisely, one thousand six hundred guns thundered into action, shattering the night calm. As far as the waiting men could see, the mountains were burning. Against the background of flames, it almost seemed as if the great earth masses had begun to dance under the weight of their fire. Ten minutes – twenty – thirty. The valleys and ravines echoed and re-echoed to the tremendous thunder of the guns. Forty-five minutes. Suddenly all fell silent. Then the whistles began to shrill. Officers shouted orders. NCOs cursed angrily. The waiting infantry stood up from the protection of the olive trees. The tanks took up their positions at the heads of the columns. The great khaki wave, designed to swamp the German Cassino Front once and for all, began to roll.

SEVEN

Dawn came at last. It had been a terrible night for the men of Wotan. The Poles – their new attackers – had come marching out of the wall of smoke in solid khaki ranks, bugles blowing, eagle banners flying. They had stopped them less than fifty metres from their perimeter. Polish dead were piled up a metre deep in front of the Wotan's positions. But they had come again. This time the Wotan had only managed to stop them when they were within a grenade's distance of the first foxhole line.

An hour before dawn they had tried once more. The exhausted SS men had ucceeded in halting them. But this time the Poles did not fall back down the hillside as before. Under the cover of a concentrated mortar barrage, they dug their heels in. With their bayonets, helmets, canteens – bare hands – they scraped shallow holes in the hard stony soil and fought on. Now, as the sun started to slide up over the mountains, their dead littered the whole hillside. But they were no less than twenty metres from the Wotan's out perimeter.

Dawn brought other problems. While the Poles contained the Wotan with a steady stream of mortar and machine-gun fire, another enemy began to slip into the German's positions from the peak. All night their patrols had wormed their way through the minefield, digging out the deadly 'deballockers'. Now the rest of the *burnous*-clad French Goumiers stole through the paths the patrols had cleared, the first rays of the sun sparkling on their knives.

General Juin, the French Army Commander, had unleashed twelve thousand of them on the Cassino front.

'Their method of working is similar to the action of an incoming tide on a series of sand castles, *Mon général*,' he had explained to Clark three days before. 'My Goumiers move up silently on any opposition, concentrate, dispose of it, and disperse again to deal with the next one. And the only sign of their passing is that their dead enemies are minus their heads. You see, my Goumiers like to bring back tangible evidence that they have carried out their orders.' He had shrugged. 'Unpleasant, possibly, but it puts the fear of God into the Boches!'

Now the first company crept from the rocks towards the Twin Tit position, their feet bare to make no noise, their set and determined faces dark beneath their turbans. Lieutenant Bogex, their commander, knew they were out for blood.

Sergeant Metzger had volunteered to do the dawn spell of sentry duty at the CP. During the night he preferred to cower in the deepest corner of the well-protected command bunker. Dawn, as he saw it, was the safest time of the day during a battle; at least you could see your enemy – and there was always the possibility of getting a bit of extra food because the dawn sentry was in charge of cooking the breakfast.

Now he leaned against the rock on which he had mounted the CP's spandau, half listening to the battle on the other side of the perimeter, half dozing. Time and time again he had to force his eyes open to prevent himself falling into a deep sleep. All night long he had not been able to sleep: the possibility of the Poles' breaking through had kept him awake and quaking at the thought of a grenade coming through the open door of the bunker, followed by squat, flat-faced Polacks spraying the men inside with tommy guns.

The eastern sky was glowing red now. Metzger yawned. The arsehole of the world – Cassino – looked almost beautiful this morning. He yawned again; he shoved his helmet to the back of his head and lit the stump of his last cigar. With a sigh of contentment he breathed out a stream of blue smoke. He thought of his wife Lore. He wondered where she was this morning? His face grew grim.

'She'd better be in her own bed with her legs shut tight!' he said half aloud in a thick voice coarsened by years of cheap *Kron* and bellowing at recruits on barrack squares. 'I don't want her giving it away to any of them rear echelon stallions.' His grim look softened, as he fell to recollecting Lore's ample charms. She had not really been the right wife for the proud holder of the SS's senior non-commissioned rank in its premier formation, the Wotan; but she had a superb body. 'Legs right up to her sweet little arse,' he told himself and puffed a little more rapidly on his cheap ten pfennig cigar.

'*Là*!' Bogex whispered and pointed to the thin pillar of blue smoke rising from behind the boulder. 'Sentry!'

Sergeant Achmed and Corporal Abou smiled. To Bogex they seemed to have more teeth than normal people. He shuddered. He wouldn't like to fall into their hands. But they were damn good irregular fighters – and they were expendable; there were thousands of them still in Morocco ready to die for *La Belle France*, for a few sous a day and as much plunder as they could carry in their infantry packs.

The two Africans hushed forward. Their skinny brown feet did not seem to feel the cruelly sharp rocks. Bogex watched as they crept closer to the Boche position. Once they had knocked out the sentry, he would rush their main bunker. With luck he could do it before they tumbled to the fact that they were being attacked. Now the Goumiers were crouched behind the rock. Achmed stuck his long curved knife between his teeth. He sought and found a stone. He nodded to Corporal Abou. Achmed tossed the stone to the right of the boulder. In the same instant Abou moved swiftly to its left.

They caught Sergeant Metzger by complete surprise. As he turned startled, to the right, his heart beating suddenly like a trip-hammer, the brown arm snaked round his neck. His cigar-stump popped out of his mouth and his shriek was stifled instantly. Something sharp stuck into his ribs. In a flash there were dark, hawk-faced men all around him, breathing their garlic breath into his face.

'Comrade ... comrade,' he quavered, feeling the hot urine trickling down his leg into his dice-beaker*.

Roughly Abou propelled him forward towards Bogex, his boots, full of urine, squelching as he did so.

'Quoi, mon Lieutenant?' Abou asked gutturally.

Bogex, preparing for the rush on the bunker, drew his forefinger across his throat. Metzger's face went ashen-grey.

* SS slang for jackboot (*transl.*).

'No, no. I'm a cripple!' he pleaded, holding up his mutilated hand, the souvenir of Russia, which had saved him from front-line combat duty ever since. Bogex spat drily in the dust.

'SS,' he said contemptuously, looking up at the panic-stricken Sergeant, 'I've shit 'em! *Allons!*' he whispered, '*allons et vivent les goumiers!*'

As the North African irregulars streamed forward silently to attack the Twin Tits position, Abou slit Metzger's throat with deliberate, unhurried calm. The former butcher boy could not have done the job better himself. Abou allowed him to sink to the blood-stained dirt. Swiftly he rifled the German's pocket. He found nothing save an Italian pornographic magazine. But Abou wasn't interested in women, unless there was nothing better available. He spat into Metzger's face and ripping open his flies, began to wield his knife swiftly and expertly on the German's loins. Within seconds he was finished and stowing his bloody souvenir in his pack. Silently he ran after the rest, leaving Sergeant Metzger to die, minus that organ of which he had once been so inordinately proud.

'Five women I used to keep satisfied at one time,' he had been wont to boast to his cronies of the Sergeants' Mess, 'and one of them a doctor's wife – and you all know what dirty pigs *they* are in bed!'

But another veteran of the SS Assault Battalion Wotan* Captain Schwarz did not fail his duty that dawn. He had just groped his way out of the still sleeping bunker, latrine paper in his good hand, when he heard Metzger's last dying gasp as Abou emasculated him. He could not identify its cause, but he could interpret its significance. The Amis had somehow or other worked their way through the minefield! Schwarz did not hesitate a second. Grabbing his machine-pistol he sprang into the latrine pit. His dark Jewish eyes gleaming crazily, he screamed: '*Alarm ... alarm,*' and fired a burst into the crouched, running ranks of the Goumiers. The Vulture, helmetless and without his monocle, swung himself behind the sole remaining recoilless rifle, assisted by a trembling Creeper. The first shell blew a great hole in the Africans' ranks. Bogex went

* See Leo Kessler: *SS Panzer Battalion* for further details.

down. Abou and Achmed fell with him, their hawklike faces impassive even in the moment of death. Still the Africans came on.

But the three officers held them. Knee-deep in stinking faeces, Schwarz swung his Schmeisser from left to right in a deadly arc. The Vulture pumped shell after shell at the Africans over open sights. Each one tore the attackers to pieces. But they did not surrender. They ran bare-footed at the German position time and time again to be slaughtered, their coal-black eyes gleaming in the frenzy of death; and it was only when the sound of running boots told them that reinforcements were arriving from the perimeter that they broke off their attack. Sullenly, they backed into the rocks from which they had come bending every now and again to pick up their fallen comrades' packs. Their dead and wounded could fend for themselves, but the loot could not be abandoned. Finally as a panting von Dodenburg appeared with his gasping, leaden-lunged section, they withdrew for good, and there was no need for his aid.

The Vulture slumped down on the rock behind the gun, while Schwarz clambered out of the latrine pit, his boots encrusted with faeces. Geier fought to control his hectic breathing:

'Damn close thing, von Dodenburg,' he said. 'Damn close.'

But if he had managed to control his breathing, he could not control his hands. As he finally rose to his feet, von Dodenburg's eyes fell on them. They were trembling violently. The Vulture was mortally afraid.

The Peak became a graveyard for the young men of the Wotan. The foxholes were heaped with their bodies. When the survivors stood on them, cries escaped from their open mouths; it was the gas escaping from their bellies, bloated in the warm Italian sun. Rats the size of cats were everywhere. The wounded near Twin Tits had to be given revolvers to fight them off. If they failed, they woke up to find them gnawing at their toes, fingers, even their noses.

The whole perimeter was heavy with the sickly sweet stench of the dead and the dying. Those who could still stand and fight wore dirty rags soaked in *grappa* to ward off the smell. Otherwise they retched continually with dry, body-racking sobs that left them green and shaking. And still the enemy attacked. They no longer knew their nationality. Their attackers had become one amorphous mass, intent on wiping them off the face of the earth, dying in their scores, crying out in half a dozen European languages.

The stream, their sole source of water was captured, its course full of bloated corpses. They drank the stagnant, green-scummed water from the shell-holes, fighting off the rats which infested them with hand grenades. Their food began to run out. At night when the shelling had died down, they crawled out into no-man's land and robbed the dead Tommies of their bully-beef and biscuits.

'The best grub I've ever tasted,' Schulze cried, gulping down the stuff, his filthy hands covered with grease, the biscuit sticking to the thick stubble on his chin. 'Nothing like it in this world!'

He spent the rest of the night spewing his guts up. The dead Tommy's hand from which he had torn it, was alive with maggots.

The enemy brought up light tanks. How they ever got them up the slope, the red-eyed, exhausted Wotan men neither knew nor cared. Suddenly they were there, churning up the bodies of their fallen, as they crawled over them in low gear, their tracks covered in blood, whipping new life into the dead, making their arms and legs flail in ghastly motion.

Their recoilless rifle had gone. Knocked out long ago. Screaming troopers rushed forward armed with *grappa* bottles filled with petrol, the rags being used as wicks burning brightly. One after another the tanks went up in flames. So did the troopers, dodging back too late as the flames roared up. Screaming men, burning oil and petrol, the nauseating stench of burned flesh.

When the enemy were not attacking, the shells plastered them. A man fell, fountains of blood spurting up in the sunshine where his head had been. An NCO lying in a shell-hole, trying to stuff his guts back into the hole that was his belly and dying with his hands buried deep inside him. An officer running panic-stricken across the ever-shrinking perimeter, dragging his guts behind him like a monstrous worm. And at the end of one such bombardment, the single shot of the big Bavarian surgeon committing suicide because all his supplies had run out. Besides, his left hand had just been severed by a shell fragment.

Occasionally they had a breather – a minute, an hour – they did not know. Time had no meaning for them now. Death had placed his hand on their shoulders and there were no more places to run. Their salvation was to accept his cold and final embrace and get it over with. On the morning of the third day, von Dodenburg found that two of his men had not responded to the weary order to 'stand to'. One had removed his boot, hooked his big toe in the rifle guard and wedged its muzzle under his chin; there was not much left of his face. The other had slit his wrists with a razor-blade.

Slowly, but inevitably, the Tommies, the Polacks, the Niggers started to push them back. At the end of the fourth day they were down to two hundred men unwounded and their perimeter wasn't much bigger than a couple of pre-war football pitches. At the end of the fifth it was one football pitch, held by a hundred weary men. The ammunition began to run out. The end on Peak 555 was not far off now. On the morning of the sixth day – to the accompaniment of the belch and plop of the Tommies' 3-inch mortaring softening them up for yet another attack – the Vulture called the officers of Battle Group Wotan together for his last conference. There were exactly four of them: the Vulture, the Creeper, Captain Schwarz and von Dodenburg – four survivors out of forty.

'Gentlemen.' The Vulture began exactly as he had always begun a conference since von Dodenburg first joined Wotan four years before as a young lieutenant. But the harsh Prussian rasp had gone from his voice now. 'I – we – have to make a decision.'

A mortar bomb landed close by, and the bunker shook like a ship hitting a trough in the waves. The Hindenburg Light*

* A thick, long burning candle, first invented in World War II and named after FM Hindenburg (*transl.*).

flickered wildly and cast its shadows in monstrous relief on to the dirt wall.

'You were saying, sir?' Schwarz was nursing his wooden arm as if he could still feel pain in it.

The Vulture licked his scummed lips as if he were not only afraid, but also embarrassed. 'Well, we . . . we must evacuate the perimeter – evacuate the whole peak.'

If he had expected any reaction to the announcement, he didn't get it. They all knew that there was no other way out if they wished to save the handful of men still alive. Besides, Peak 555 had no military value left now. The Cassino line was about finished. The Tommies were already well lodged on Monte Cassino itself. It would be only a matter of hours before they took the ruin itself.

'I see you expected the decision.'

Von Dodenburg nodded.

'The problem is how we are going to evacuate the men. I've got fifty—' he shrugged – 'perhaps sixty walking wounded. The rest will have to take their chance that the Tommies beat the Polacks up here. The Tommies may not shoot them, but the Polacks will. And I've got some forty men still capable of fighting.'

Schwarz let go of his wooden arm.

'We've got roughly the same number around the CP, sir,' he snapped. 'But we can't move them until—'

The Vulture held up his hand. 'There is a slight technical problem.' He paused. Outside their spandaus belted lead into the Poles in short rationed bursts. In the pauses, von Dodenburg could even hear the guttural Slavic sounds of their officers' orders. 'You see, all of us are not coming out.' The Vulture lowered his eyes as if he did not wish to see their dismay.

'Not all of us,' Schwarz broke the silence. 'May I volunteer to stay behind with the rearguard?'

'It is not a matter of a rearguard, Schwarz,' the Vulture said carefully. 'You see, I have Smiling Albert's permission to take out a few men who will form the cadre of a new Battle Group Wotan, to be formed in the Homeland with this summer's seventeen year olds. I shall select the members of that cadre who will be picked up in an hour's time by Kesselring's two personal Fieseler Storchs. They will land behind the CP. For that reason we must hold on to this position to the last.'

Von Dodenburg let the Vulture's words die away while he did a rapid calculation. Two Fieseler Storchs – that would mean a dozen men at the most.

'*Just twelve of us!*' he interrupted, 'but that would mean the end of the Wotan!'

'Yes,' the Vulture said, 'that figure would be about right – twelve key men to ensure that our old tradition is carried on in the new Group.'

'And who are you going to take?' von Dodenburg asked, his hand falling to his holster.

The gesture did not escape the Vulture. He licked his lips. Outside the Poles were falling back once again.

'Men whom I think would be the most valuable. You, for instance, my dear Major. If—'

'Yes, I, for instance,' von Dodenburg cut him short, 'if I became your creature.'

He never finished the accusation. The Creeper elbowed him to one side, his face tense with fear.

'And me, Colonel? I promise you absolute loyalty. Forget the past. I'm yours. You can trust me, sir.'

'Keep your damned Gestapo spy paws off me!' the Vulture barked. 'I want none of your kind of arse-crawling toadies with me!' He turned to von Dodenburg. 'Well, this is the last time, von Dodenburg, you've got to make your decision – are you with us or not?'

The two men faced each other tensely.

'Well?' the Vulture demanded, iron in his voice. 'Your last chance.

'I wouldn't care if refusal meant condemnation to hell,' von Dodenburg retorted contemptuously. 'I want no part of your treacherous schemes—'

'Treacherous schemes?' Schwarz interrupted.

But neither of the two men facing each other in this final confrontation paid any attention to him. Both knew that this was the parting of the ways after four long years of war together. They had come far: the capture of the great fort of Eben Emael in forty; the glorious push through France; the first day of Barbarossa in forty-one; Russia; the last great armoured push against the Ivans at Kursk in forty-three; and this. Slowly von Dodenburg began to draw his pistol.

'What are you going to do, Major?' the Vulture asked slowly.

'You are a traitor, Colonel Geier,' he replied, no rage in his heart, only the knowledge that he must carry out his duty. 'You are prepared to betray our folk-comrades for your own petty safety.'

'But, you damn young fool, von Dodenburg!' the Vulture cried exasperatedly, his eyes fixed on the pistol in the other officer's hand. 'I'm doing this for Germany ... I'm trying to save her from those men who will sacrifice her without compunction. When they go down, they will drag the rest down with them. Don't you understand – what I am trying to do is for our Homeland!'

Coldly von Dodenburg cocked his pistol, his face expressionless. The Vulture backed away. His hand fell to his belt. But before he could reach his holster, von Dodenburg had jerked up his pistol threateningly. His knuckle whitened as it slid around the trigger of the pistol and took the pressure. The Vulture's adam's apple moved back and forth as he swallowed painfully.

'Von Dodenburg!!'

Von Dodenburg began to raise his pistol. The Vulture's face seemed to shrink. His hands flew to his chin, as if he hoped to ward off the bullets with the naked flesh.

'Colonel, I'll help, if you'll take me with you.'

It was Kriecher. With a grunt of rage he flung himself at von Dodenburg. Automatically von Dodenburg pressed the trigger. The Vulture was thrown off his feet. His body smashed against the dirt wall. His eyes filled with disbelief as he looked down at the gaping wound amidst the decorations which he had sacrificed so many good men's lives to gain.

The Creeper scrambled forward and clutched the Vulture's boots.

'It was a mistake, Colonel,' he whispered, his face contorted with fear. 'You must believe me – a mistake!'

Schwarz hit the Creeper with his wooden arm. Blood gushed

from his nose and ears as he fell backwards. Schwarz kicked him in the crotch. He gave a thin scream, stifled by the vomit which flooded his throat. The next instant, Schwarz's slug smashed his skull. The Vulture looked down at the mangled face and at his boots splashed with the dead Kriecher's brains and blood. As the sounds of the Tommy mortar barrage started to be drowned by the roar of an airplane motor, Colonel Geier of the Wotan slid to the dirt floor, twitched once and lay still. The Vulture was dead.

Four: The Breakout

'We don't want you . . . Wotan does not need you. We fight on!'

Major von Dodenburg to Captain Wagner.

ONE

'Holy shit,' Wagner breathed in awe. 'Is the front always like this?'

Ertz, the pilot nodded.

'Yes, Captain. No fancy uniforms out here – and another glass of champus, General? This is how the front swine live.'

As the little observation plane began to lose height over the embattled peak, Schellenberg's fellow plotter could see the dead bodies piled high, their limbs twisted grotesquely. Everywhere there were the charred, shattered wrecks of tanks and vehicles, trails of abandoned weapons up the mountainside, and always bodies – bodies without heads, bodies without arms, bodies without legs. The yellow Italian soil was soaked red with their blood. Wagner licked his lips.

'Do you think you can make it, Ertz?' he asked, as the plane seemed to hover over the peak, while the pilot sized up the situation. Ertz held up his gloved thumb confidently.

'Sure. I've tackled worse as pissed as ten naked niggers. I'll come in with that peak on my tail. At least it'll keep the Tommies from shooting me up the arse and it might slow my landing speed. I'll have no tail wind, you see.' He peered at the perimeter some four hundred feet below. 'I might just be able to catch the bitch before we roll into the Tommy lines – in time for China tea, eh?'

Wagner gulped as the pilot pulled back the stick and soared upwards towards the peak. Behind them, Smiling Albert's other plane followed suit.

The big SS Captain was scared, very scared; but he knew how vital it was for the success of their plot to get the Vulture and his key – and loyal – officers out now. Adolf Hitler had been so impressed by their stand on the Peak and the tremendous propaganda success of the bombing of Monte Cassino by the Amis that he had fully approved the scheme to get the Vulture off the mountain-top. Indeed he had ordered that the Vulture should reform his Battle Group in Berlin itself. Based at Spandau with some three thousand idealistic youngsters under his command, the Vulture would play a decisive role in their seizure of power in the capital. Wagner fought back his fear. They had to get down.

The first Storch came in low to their rear. Ertz had cut the engine and was gliding in silently. The Tommies dug in behind the peak heard him only when it was too late. He was over their heads and gone before they could open fire. When they did, their tracer missed the German plane by metres.

Schulze spotted the little plane first.

'Sir,' he yelled, 'the Storch!' Von Dodenburg swung round and focused his eyes against the slanting rays of the sun. There it was – a stark black silhouette against the red ball of the sun. The rest of the traitors had arrived.

Something snapped in the young Major's brain. He was seized by a burning rage. As the little plane came closer and closer, he unslung his machine-pistol. Legs set wide apart, he fired a furious burst at the plane. The slugs were wide of the mark. But they had their effect. The Storch's motor burst into life suddenly and with an abrupt turn of speed, it zoomed up into the sky above their heads.

'Great crap on the Christmas Tree!' Wagner gasped, the sweat standing out on his brow in heavy beads. 'What the hell are they firing on us for? Can't they see the black crosses?'

Ertz breathed out a sigh of relief as he gained control of the bucking plane, caught in one of the peak's thermals. 'I always thought those stubble-hoppers were a bit thick – perhaps they're so front-happy, they don't know what side they're on!'

Wagner's brain was racing. He was damned scared. But he knew he had to go through with the mission. If he didn't, Schellenberg would have no compunction about sending him to the front – or worse.

'Listen,' he said urgently, 'go in again, Ertz. Under power this time.' He opened the flap of the side window. A blast of icy air gushed in. Wagner seized one of the grenades which all the planes carried to destroy vital or secret equipment in case they had to force-land behind enemy lines, and held it out of the window in readiness.

'I'm going to clear that stupid turd out of the way – even if I have to kill the bastard.'

Ertz shrugged carelessly.

'Why not? Let's kill a few of our own stubble-hoppers and put them out of their misery. Anything for a change, eh?' He gave the little wooden plane full power and they came zooming down once more.

Von Dodenburg waited, while Schulze stared at him aghast. He had never seen the Major like this: he seemed to have gone temporarily *meschugge.**

'Sir,' he cried, 'let's get our arses out of here smartish! The Tommies'll be zeroing in on us in a minute! *Sir!*'

The Major did not hear. His eyes, red with fury, were fixed on the plane roaring down at 180 km.p.h. Ertz pulled up the nose and dropped the flaps. The Storch seemed to hover momentarily in mid-air. It was Wagner's opportunity. Desperately he lobbed his grenade at the tattered, battle-worn figure standing there with the dead sprawled out extravagantly around him.

'Get out of the way, you crazy fool!' he yelled.

The grenade came sailing down – a deadly little black egg from the hovering bird. It exploded with a harsh crump. Chunks of metal hissed through the air. Schulze yelped with

* Yiddish for 'crazy', commonly used in the SS (*transl.*).

pain as a fragment hit him in the shoulder. But von Dodenburg did not falter. The air was filled with the stink of petrol. The plane was almost on them now. He could see the two white faces behind the gleam of the perspex quite clearly. He raised his Schmeisser.

'*We don't want you!*' he screamed. '*Wotan does not need you – we fight on!*'

The plane seemed about to crash directly into him. The roar was ear-splitting. Schulze ducked. And in that instant, von Dodenburg fired a full burst. The vicious red tracers stitched a line of deadly holes across the fuselage. They struck the perspex. It smashed at once. The two white faces disappeared behind a spiderweb of cracked gleaming perspex. The pilot threw up his hands in front of his face in horror.

'Holy Christ, you've shot him down!' Schulze yelled.

At two hundred kilometres an hour, the blinded plane careened over the perimeter, thick white smoke pouring from its punctured engine. Desperately Ertz tried to fight it down. The port tyre hit the rock first. It burst like an 88 shell exploding. The Storch lurched violently. Its port wing hit the ground. There was a rending sound. The Storch shimmied crazily. Ertz battled with the controls. Great clouds of dust shot up on both sides. With Wagner screaming hysterically at his side, they crashed into one of the abandoned tanks. The next instant they were crushed to death as the plane folded like a concertina.

On the perimeter the awe-struck German and Allied watchers ducked as a solitary wheel flew, still revolving, through the air. A moment later the Storch exploded and the two SS men were running wildly for the Twin Tits bunker before the Allies came out of their trance and started firing at them.

Schulze cast a curious glance at the blood-stained bodies of the Creeper and the Vulture bundled into the corner of the littered bunker. But he said nothing. Instead he turned his attention to von Dodenburg, who was now apparently recovering from the red-eyed rage which had overcome him outside.

'They've gone – the planes,' he said to Schwarz, slumped wearily at the table, heaped high with open ration cans and boxes of ammunition. 'We're on our own, Schwarz.'

'I see,' the one-armed Captain said tonelessly. 'And now?'

'There are going to be no privileged persons in Wotan,' von Dodenburg snapped. 'We all take the same chances now. We are going to break out, Schwarz – at the earliest possible opportunity. We won't last another day here and' – he hesitated. 'Germany has need of the Wotan.'

'But how are we going to do it, sir?' Schulze asked. 'The Tommies have got us by the short and curlies – that's for sure.'

Von Dodenburg swept a pile of empty cans of 'Old Man' off the rough table made of ration cases and spread out his dirty map.

'The perimeter,' he jabbed a forefinger at the centre of the map. 'Now reduced to perhaps a hundred odd square metres. The Tommies dug in in force – here, here and here. Our last defensible position – here. The Twin Tits, some seventy metres from the thinnest section of the Tommy line.' Schulze, always quick to react, blurted it out:

'So that's the way out, sir?'

'Right in one, Schulze.'

'But it is still too strongly held for our men – lions that they are – to break through,' Schwarz objected, his face as impassive as ever, utterly unafraid. For him the breakout was not a matter of life and death. His sole concern was whether or not the breakout was militarily feasible.

'I agree. But you must agree too that the Peak section of the enemy line is the thinnest held. If we are going to get out, it must be through that section. But how?' Von Dodenburg gave them a tired smile. 'Our sole remaining ace up the sleeve – the Goliath!'

'The Goliath!' Schulze exploded joyously. 'Of course, the Goliath. I'd forgotten about that!'

Just before they had flown from Tempelhof, a special messenger had arrived from the Berlin Arsenal: a bespectacled, fat Major of Artillery.

'The Führer's compliments, Major,' he had announced after a sloppy exchange of salutes. 'He wishes you to have the honour of trying out first another of our nation's secret weapons.' Against the background of the old Auntie Ju's three roaring engines, he had taken the mystified SS men to the back of the Opel truck and had thrown back the flaps to reveal what looked like a Mark III tank reduced to nursery proportions.

'What the hell's that, Major?' Schulze had blurted out. 'Does the Führer want us to fight the rest of the war with kids' toys?'

The middle-aged Major, his fat chest decorated solely with the War Service Cross, Third Class, had been in no way offended.

'That toy, soldier,' he had answered, 'contains one ton of high explosive which can be steered to the enemy lines by remote control. One day our newest little toy might well save your life.'

Schulze realized that that day had now come.

'You mean, sir, we use it to blast a hole through the Tommies' line?'

Von Dodenburg nodded.

'Almost right. But there is one slight difference in my plan. It's this. We use the Goliath as a feint. It's got one weakness, you know – it's slow and noisy. The Tommies will hear it coming. They will be alerted. All right, so what do we do? We use it as a feint, while we slip through their line here.'

Schulze peered over his shoulder at the map.

'Bit rough, isn't it, sir? Cliff face and all.'

'The place most likely to be weakly held!'

'Of course, of course, von Dodenburg,' Schwarz agreed. 'A capital plan. And when?'

'As soon as it grows dark. We shall withdraw the men now and form a hedgehog around this bunker.* This will be the starting point for our breakout.'

'And the wounded, sir?' Schulze asked.

'If they can walk and carry a rifle, they come with us.'

'And if they can't?'

'Then they stay.' He turned his gaze on the big Hamburger, his light blue eyes harder than Schulze ever remembered seeing them before. 'The Wotan cannot afford itself the luxury of pity any more.'

* Typical SS defensive position (*transl.*).

TWO

It was the sledgehammer of the shell-booms coming time and time again that brought terror to the survivors' souls. All afternoon the Tommies had been pounding the tiny bloody perimeter before the last attack. Now von Dodenburg could see that the men were just about finished. Their pits were filled with the mortally wounded and the shattered ground was littered with their dead whom the shells did not leave in peace even after death. As for the living, he could see the flesh around their blood-scummed lips quivering. Their eyes were coated with a hot sheen, as if tears were close and the blood had drained from their pinched faces.

But the tremendous pounding went on, while the sun defiantly refused to slide beyond the mountain and grant them the blessing of darkness. Now the young men had become old. The only human sounds they uttered were cries of pain and prayers to gods they had long forgotten. The rest was a kind of animal whimpering. A corporal with both his legs shot off crawled along on the bloody stumps begging someone to shoot him. But no one had the strength any more to do so. Major von Dodenburg knew that they had reached breaking point.

'Goddammit,' he cried impotently, his fist clenched, 'for God's sake, sun – go down!'

He scrambled wildly through the tremendous bombardment to the foremost bunker, the closest to the Peak. The handful of young SS men holding it were finished. They had absorbed too many shells, seen too many torn bodies, suffered too much fear. Their faces were blank, but their twitching lips and dilated eyes revealed the extent of their breakdown. One had filled his field grey pants. The stench was overpowering, but neither he nor the others seemed to notice.

Von Dodenburg flung himself down beside Schulze. Time and time again, their helmets were showered by dirt and rock thrown up by the exploding shells. Von Dodenburg would have liked to have screamed, buried himself at the bottom of the pit, evacuated his bowels – anything to escape the unbearable strain of the bombardment. But his rigid sense of duty made him face up to the task ahead of him. He would save these shivering broken wrecks of men despite themselves.

He focused his glasses, a piece of paper shading the tops of the lenses to prevent their gleam in the setting sun from giving away his position. A hundred metres to his right was the start of the scrub covered cliff. In front of it he could make out what looked like a machine-gun pit, covered by half a dozen infantry foxholes. That had to be their point of his escape. But where would he launch his Goliath? It was armoured well enough. But a direct hit, say by a mortar bomb, would put it out of action and he couldn't risk that. He swept the area with his glasses. Then he gave a gasp of horror. A body loomed into view. It had been sliced lengthwise, leaving the corpse an uncanny half-man. But coming from the massive wound, there stretched an apparently endless length of intestine. The ghastly rope of flesh dappled by the sinking sun, lay like a marker tape just in front of the most heavily defended part of the Tommies' front. He lowered his glasses. The Goliath attack would go in at 'Half-man's Point'.

Von Dodenburg fired his last flare. The green light hushed into the darkening sky. A few metres away, Schulze pressed the power button. Slowly the secret weapon nosed its way out of the cover of the forward bunker and began to climb over the pile of rubble, silent save for the slight rattle of well-oiled tracks.

'Jesus H—' Schulze whispered to himself, as he started to steer it towards Half-man's Point, 'puts the wind right up you!'

Still the Tommies had not noticed the ton of high explosive heading in their direction. Perhaps the noise of bombardment drowned the sound; perhaps they were too busy preparing for their own attack which would go in as soon as the bombardment ended. Metre by metre it crawled forward, only just visible in the ever-growing darkness, sensing its way over and around the obstacles of the shell-pitted no-man's land. It was almost as if it had a life of its own. Von Dodenburg felt the small hairs at the back of his neck rising. There was something uncanny about the Goliath as it crawled towards the enemy, bearing its deadly gift.

It detected the half-man. It hesitated for an instant. But it did not attempt to avoid him. It simply rolled over the corpse. Von Dodenburg shuddered. He felt sure he had heard the ghastly ribbon of gut hanging from the body squash under its weight. Suddenly there was a yell of alarm.

'Hey, lads, what do you make of that?' The Tommy line was too dark for him to see the face of the speaker, but he could imagine it: shocked and puzzled. How would they react now?

With his free hand, von Dodenburg signalled the survivors to prepare for their dash forward to the peak. There was a single shot from the enemy lines. He heard the slug whine off the Goliath's armour.

'Good God,' he prayed to himself fervently, 'don't let them use artillery!'

'What do you make of the bugger?' a coarse voice floated across.

'Search me, mate. Who do you think I am – sodding Jesus Christ?'

'Give it a burst of bren,' a third voice suggested.

The slow British machine-gun chattered. The morse of a tracer burst zipped across the night sky. Still the Goliath came on. Someone screamed:

'Where's the sodding mortar platoon? You can never find the bastards when you want them. Sergeant, where's—'

His words were drowned in the roar. A huge spurt of red flame tore the darkness apart. In its blood-red light von Dodenburg could see the bodies flying into the sky. The Goliath had hit the Tommies' line! He sprang to his feet, Schmeisser at the ready.

'Battle Group Wotan,' he yelled at the top of his voice above the screams of pain from the Tommy side, 'Follow me!'

They streamed after him, firing as they ran. The Tommies were in complete chaos. Von Dodenburg saw one of his men stumble over the body of one Tommy he had just shot. Before he could right himself, the wounded Tommy pulled out a grenade and blew them both sky-high. But that was their only casualty. The enemy machine-gun was knocked out before it could open fire, the gunners scattering under the rush. A couple of the covering infantry sprang out of their pits and tried to hold them. But they were bayoneted before they knew what hit them. Within a matter of seconds they had burst through the Tommies' positions and were running, leaden-lunged and gasping frantically, for the dark cliff ahead.

The climb was easier than they had anticipated. They lost only one man, who slipped, clutching frantically at a patch of coarse scrub which held him for an instant before being torn out of the stony soil and plunging him screaming with fear into the red-splashed, confused darkness below.

The steep slope downwards into the darkness and the safety of their own lines beyond proved different. Their chests heaving with the effort, their breath coming in broken harsh gasps, the survivors stared numbly at the void below their feet.

'Heaven, arse and twine,' von Dodenburg rounded on them. 'What's the matter with you? Do you want me to carry you down on my back? For Christ sake, get a move on, the Tommies will be up here after us at any moment!'

'Time to go!' Schulze yelled and flung himself over the top. He disappeared into the darkness in a shower of dust and rocks. 'Come on,' his voice trailed after him. 'You'll get the para's badge for this one – without a parachute.'

The sudden burst of machine-gun fire somewhere to their rear, followed by an angry shout, did the rest. In a miniature landslide, they sprang over the side and down the steep slope. Some slid down on their rear and tore their pants to shreds. Others grabbed madly at the olive trees and thick shrubs as they raced down, nearly wrenching their arms from their sockets whenever they managed to get a hold. But down they went, following Schulze's laughter floating up from below.

One by one they crashed to a stop at the bottom. Von Dodenburg went face first into a tree. He felt his nose smash. But he did not care. They had managed the first stage successfully. He shook his head to clear it and wiped the blood away with his sleeve.

'All right,' he said, thickly, his mouth full of blood. 'No time for hanging about. By dawn we want to clear this damned mountain completely. Or we're sitting ducks. Now it's march or croak, lads.'

He slung his machine-pistol and stepped out. The long march from the mountain to the rear had begun.

It was a strange night, full of alarms and sudden frights. On all sides they heard the snap and crackle of the intensive fire-fight which was reaching its crescendo now, as the full weight of the enemy attack was flung in on the sacred mountain. The covering Peak 555 had gone; now all that was left was Monte Cassino. More than once they heard German spoken close by. But von Dodenburg did not allow them to stop. Wotan would fend for itself. Twice they ran into the reserve positions of the Poles who were now within rifle-shot of the shattered Monastery and they had to clear them at bayonet-point.

A line of undefended barbed-wire entanglements barred their way – whether they had been built by the Germans or the enemy, they did not know. But they seemed to stretch for kilometres to right and left; and von Dodenburg knew there was no time to reconnoitre. They took a chance and blew them with their last bangalore torpedo. The explosion shattered the night into a thousand fiery splinters. But no angry shouts in a foreign tongue followed, and they ran unharmed through the reeking gap in the barrier.

They followed a track of loose stones, sheltered by a rough stone wall. It led them to a ruined house. But it was occupied all right. Crouched in the darkness, hardly daring to breathe, they could see the yellow light coming from one of the battered windows and could hear the sound of a woman's laughter

'Well, I'll be buggered,' Schulze cursed softly. 'A shitting mobile whore-house!' He cocked his head to one side. 'And listen to them bedsprings – going like a Yiddish fiddler's elbow!' He liked his lips longingly.

Von Dodenburg nudged him in the ribs. 'Come on Casanova, there'll be time enough for that when and if we get out of this!'

Schulze sighed.

'It's a sore temptation, sir. So close – all hot and steaming – and yet so far.'

Von Dodenburg chuckled and led them cautiously past the strange house.

The hours passed. They stumbled on slowly, hanging on to the tunic of the man in front, only kept on their feet by their desire to escape and von Dodenburg's inspired leadership. Now, he, Schulze and Schwarz, bringing up the rear, were carrying three rifles, each of soldiers too weary to bear the weight themselves. Kilometre after kilometre. The rattle of the small arms fire grew fainter. Now the only sound was the steady rumble of the heavies pounding the flaming peak of Monte Cassino. But the burning mountain, soon to be consumed by the Allied fire, served its purpose for them. For von Dodenburg in the lead it acted as a bearing. But even as he marched northwards, he realized that those flames which guided them also symbolized the end of Germany's hopes in the south of Italy. The Cassino Front was finished. Now the great race for Rome would begin. And from there? Who knew? One thing was certain, he told himself, biting back the pain of his blistered feet and his broken nose, Wotan would never be wasted again. Whenever the elite of the SS were used again, he would ensure that they would be employed only in the decisive battles. They had gone through too much to be thrown away at the whim of the men in Berlin. From now onwards, he would decided on their employment.

'If we are to dig our own graves,' he whispered to himself, his teeth gritted with pain, 'we shall make our own decisions where they will be . . .'

Just before dawn they began to run into well-organized defensive positions: a marked minefield, barbed wire entanglements, the first hump of a well dug-in and camouflaged forward observation post. They overcame the minefield easily, crawling along in three lines with Schulze, von Dodenburg and Schwarz prodding for the flat mines with their bayonets. They turned out to be Schuh mines.

'Do you think they are our own positions?' Schwarz asked, wiping his wooden hand across his sweat-drenched brow.

'Could be,' von Dodenburg replied. 'Anything's possible. The front is so terribly confused. But let's assume the Tommies are waiting for us at that F.O.P.* We'll take it easy.'

They pushed closer to the wire. A young corporal still had a pair of wire clippers. He crawled up to them and began to snip through the first rusty strand.

Whistles shrilled. White alarm flares hushed into the dawn sky alarmingly. The spandaus began to hiss their deadly song. Red tracer started to cut the air low over their heads; and Schulze screamed hysterically:

'We're home, lads! We're home! The shitting stubble-hoppers are just letting off a few fireworks to welcome us, that's all.'

They collected themselves behind the infantry battalion's CP. Most of them were swaying dangerously now. The stubble-hoppers had sacrificed their schnapps ration for these torn, bloody survivors of Peak 555. Its effect had been disastrous on them.

Von Dodenburg, a silly grin on his bloody face, looked at them. They were a sorry-looking lot for Germany's elite. Uniforms ripped and torn, faces covered in white dust and blood, they looked like a bunch of scarecrows. He felt his nose gingerly. It seemed twice the normal size. He looked down at his uniform. One trouser leg was gone and the sole of his right boot flapped like an extra tongue. Obviously he looked no better than his men did.

'Watch it,' he bellowed through cracked lips. The command did not seem right somehow, but it had its effect. The battered survivors of the battle for the Peak came to a semblance of the pre-attention position. 'Battalion – battalion, attention!'

'But Major,' the infantry CO cried. 'The trucks to pick you up—' The words died on his lips.

'Battalion – right turn!'

The hundred men left turned right.

'Forward – forward march!'

While the infantry gaped at them as if they were crazy, the survivors of Wotan began to limp after their officers, their pain-

* Forward Observation Post (*transl.*).

wracked faces set and determined, heads down as if they could go on for ever. The infantry Major shook his head in puzzled despair.

'The SS, gentlemen,' he murmured, turning to his officers, 'the shitting courageous SS.'

And behind them, emerging from the fog of war like some great ship, Peak 555 glowed in the sun of the new day, its summit littered with the thousand bodies of the young men from Wotan who would never rise and fight again. But the survivors limping northwards with the retreating German Army did not look back. Peak 555 was the past. However grim and uncertain, theirs was the future.

THREE

On that June 5th, the Commander of the US Fifth Army, General Mark Clark drove proudly into Rome. The Italian capital had fallen at last and he luxuriated in the applause of the crowds and the broad smiles of the sweating triumphant dogfaces, marching through on their way north, flowers sticking out of the muzzles of their Garands. Pearson, at the wheel of the General's immaculate jeep with outsize lieutenant-general's stars, grinned to himself. Clark was really enjoying this moment: the tangible sign of his breakthrough at Cassino.

Just short of the Colosseum, the crowds of screaming, flag-waving Italians made them stop momentarily.

'Goddam dagoes,' Clark muttered under his breath, but he responded to their hysterical enthusiasm with an imperial wave of his hand. Next to the jeep a young soldier in a similarly stalled infantry company took his eyes off the great Roman landmark and whistled softly:

'Jesus, General,' he said in awe, 'I didn't know that our bombers had done that much damage to Rome.'

Clark laughed. But as the mob of screaming Romans parted to allow them through, he snapped to Pearson:

'Stupid dumbell. But make a note of it, Pearson – I'll need it for my memoirs.'

'Yessir, General,' Pearson cried as he put the jeep into first. 'Roger.'

Under his breath, he muttered, '*Memoirs* – oh, my aching back!'

With Clark directing him, Pearson picked his way through the crowded streets, trying to find the Capitoline Hill, on which was located the Town Hall. Clark was intent on getting the full mileage out of his conquest. Like an old Roman General, he intended that the city should surrender itself to him formally; and behind him the next jeep was full of photographers so that the historic moment could be recorded for posterity – General Mark Clark, conqueror of Rome.

After half an hour of twisting and turning through the crowded streets, they were lost, Pearson sweating and angry, and the General very nervous. Finally they were forced to ask a shock-haired, shirt-sleeved youth the way. Thus the twentieth century conqueror of the old imperial city drove to accept its surrender, led by a teenager on an ancient racing bike, shouting excitedly for everyone to get out of the way because *il Generale Clark* was on his way to the Capitoline Hill.

Finally Pearson spotted the big balcony from which Mussolini, the deposed Duce, had once harangued his 'new Romans', who were now cheering their new master with Latin abandon. Solemnly Clark got out of his jeep and pushed his way through the crowd. He marched up the slope of the hill towards the great door of the Town Hall. The crowd fell silent. Pearson, marching stiffly behind the tall General, felt instinctively that they were awaiting some dramatic gesture from Clark. Imperiously Clark halted in front of the oaken door. He formed his fist into a club and struck it. There was a hollow boom, but nothing else. No one came to open at the command of the captain who had come three thousand miles to conquer the 'mother of all cities'. He struck another blow on it. Still no response. Angrily he seized the iron handle and turned. The door did not open.

'For Chrissake, Pearson,' he cursed, turning red-faced, 'the goddam stinking door's locked!'

'Ah well, General,' Pearson consoled the crestfallen commander, as they wandered somewhat shame-faced through the disappointed crowds back to their jeep, 'at least you've beaten General Eisenhower into France.'

Clark's craggy face brightened.

'Sure! Of course.' He chuckled softly. 'Wouldn't I give something to see Ike's face now! He sure will be riled when he sees me in the headlines all over the front pages tomorrow.'

It was June 5th, 1944. Eisenhower's great invading armada was already at sea. Tomorrow would be D-Day.

And on that same day of hollow triumph for their commander,

the Poles were collecting their dead from Peak 555 and Monte Cassino. Soon they would erect a cemetery for the four thousand who had fallen, with a memorial, which would dominate the shattered height, long after its scars had been hidden by the process of time. The inscription on it would be simple:

'We Polish soldiers
For our freedom and yours
Have given our souls to God
Our bodies to the soil of Italy.
And our hearts to Poland.'

And one hundred and fifty kilometres away, the survivors of Wotan celebrated their last day in Italy, before they returned to the Reich to reform. They spent it in the same way as they had spent every day since the breakout: drunk and in the brothels of Milan's red light district, greedily trying to make up for the lost days on the mountain.

The new Colonel von Dodenburg, commander-designate of the Wotan Battle Group, made love to the Countess Lisa for the last time. She wanted to talk. But he kissed her violently, brutally, thrusting her back on the eighteenth-century bed. He wanted to forget what must come: the blood, the stench of war, the stink of men in unwashed, battle-stained field-grey, the mass graves filled with shattered bodies.

Now his eager hands groped beneath the tight silk skirt. The expensive white blouse burst open to reveal her generous, olive-skinned breasts. He pressed his blond head to them greedily like a hungry child. She stared down at him, her dark eyes full of tears. He left her breasts with his lips. Their half-open mouths pressed together passionately. Their tongues flickered back and forth. Desire overcame him. He tore the expensive clothes and spread-eagled her on the big bed, her black underwear strewn everywhere. Her red fingernails ripped the length of his muscular back. He thrust himself between her legs. She whimpered as passion overcame her and she answered his desire. Her slim body rose and fell wildly, her mouth open, the red lips slack. And when he had finished and fallen to one side, gasping like an old man, the tears of parting flowed down her beautiful dark-skinned face, again unheeded.

In Madame Rosa's 'House of the Tight Little Whore', there was no time for love – just money. The new Senior Sergeant Schulze of Battle Group Wotan knew it too. He dumped the dirty bundle of Liri notes in front of the vast-bosomed Madame with her frizzed dyed hair piled up at least half a metre above her face.

'Money,' he said thickly, swaying dangerously, 'earned honestly by flogging what's left of our rations on the black market – before those shitting kitchen-bulls. Now,' he took another swig of the *grappa* bottle, 'where's the cunt?'

To make his meaning quite plain, he poked a dirty forefinger through a circle made with the thumb and forefinger of the other hand. If Madame Rosa did not undertand the slurred drunken flow of German, she certainly understood the money and the gesture. Her forbidding look vanished.

'I have a nice little blonde,' she said carefully. 'Only fourteen – hardly been touched. Or a dark-haired one? You Tedeschi like them dark—'

'I want *all* of 'em,' the red-faced Schulze bellowed. '*Capisce – all of 'em!*' He leaned forward and thrust an experimental hand up the Madame's skirt.

Pushing him aside irritably, the Madame clapped her plump, beringed hands.

'*Ragazzi*,' she called, 'customers.'

They came in swaying and simpering on their high heels, clad in their multi-coloured transparent *crêpe de chine* lingerie. The Madame's vast bosom seemed about to burst out of its tight black silk cage with pride.

'My girls,' she announced proudly, as they lined up in front of Schulze.

'Well, I'll go and piss up my sleeve,' Schulze breathed. 'All that meat and no potatoes! Now they're really something. All right, Mother, I'll have her,' he indicated a ripe blonde in black lace cami-knickers, 'and the one with the tits under her chin. Give me that box of Parisians there.' He picked up the box of contraceptives. 'We Prussians like to keep our powder dry, you know?' He patted the blonde on her plump, black-lace bottom. 'All right, you and your friend get yourselves upstairs and in between the sheets, ready for Daddy. But don't waste any of it before I come up.

He turned to the Madame.

'And now, madame, your high-class establishment is going to have the honour of an unofficial visit from the new NCO Corps of the Wotan Battle Group.' Before the fat Italian brothel-owner could react, he had pulled out his NCO's whistle and blown a shrill blast, the signal for the drunken, unkempt men waiting outside. The noise of their heavy, nailed dice-beakers, as they stampeded up the stone stairs, thundered like a herd of wild bulls.

A drunken corporal, his tunic torn open, his cap missing, his face covered in two days' growth of beard, dived in through a window. Ignoring the shower of smashed glass and Madame's shrieks, he inquired anxiously:

'Got it all laid on, Sergeant?

'Yes!' yelled Schulze, as they came smashing through the door, sending a flower vase flying, ripping down the heavy velvet curtains of the entrance, stumbling over the chairs, 'there's cunt for everybody.'

'But you didn't pay for this lot!' the Madame screamed.

'What's good enough for one Wotan man is good enough for them all.'

'Those men are not fit enough to fuck a pig – never mind my girls,' bellowed Madame Rosa furiously.

Without another word Schulze rammed his big docker's hand between her plump legs and lifted her on to his shoulder.

'Those lads, Rosa, are the best in the world – they deserve the best.' He heaved her to a more comfortable position. 'Come on, your old bones are going to be rattled this afternoon. Be happy you're going to get a bit of something that other women pray for at night at their bedside. And if you're good, I won't put a bag over your head after all.'

With the screaming, struggling Madame bouncing up and down on his shoulder, he ran up the stairs to the waiting whores, tears of laughter streaming down his cheeks.

They paraded at the goods station just before midnight. The Führer's special train was already there, steam rising in a thin trail from its gleaming locomotive in the yellow light of the blacked-out lamps. The chain-dogs were everywhere, their silver plates around their necks, carbines slung over their shoulders, their eyes wary and hard as they watched the veterans form up. A couple of them bore the black eyes they had received in the confused fighting at Madame Rosa's when they had tried to get Schulze's party out by force. But there was no further need for their services. The steam had gone out of the Wotan men. Now they waited, exhausted, for their commander and the order to board the special train which the Führer had sent to bring back the survivors of his premier SS regiment.

The chocolate-coloured pre-war Rolls-Royce of their CO's mistress drew up slowly at the exit. The black-suited chauffeur sprang out and opened the door for von Dodenburg. He turned to the woman nestled in the luxurious upholstery and they saw him touch his cap in farewell. Then he turned and marched stiffly to the waiting line of men. Schwarz clicked his heels together.

'Parade – *parade shun*!'

One hundred pairs of boots hit the concrete as one. They froze into rigid immobility. Schwarz swung round, strode five paces to where von Dodenburg was waiting. He halted and snapped to attention. His gloved hand touched his cap.

'Beg to report respectfully – one officer, five NCOs and one hundred and two men of Battle Group Wotan on parade, Colonel!'

'Thank you, Schwarz. Please tell the men to stand at ease.'

'At your command, Colonel!'

The dice-beakers smashed on to the concrete again. Von Dodenburg faced them in an echoing silence, broken only by the hiss of escaping steam. For a long moment, his blue eyes ran the length of their ranks. Their uniforms were shabby and stained with battle, but their chests were heavy with tin. Yet it wasn't the bronze and steel of their decorations which told him – with a thrill of recognition and pride – that these men were the best National Socialists Germany could produce: the elite of the elite. It was their gaunt, fanatical faces. And they were his – to mould into a formation which would be invincible, whatever the odds.

'Soldiers of Battle Group Wotan! Germans! *Comrades!*' he began, 'tonight we return to the Reich. Tomorrow we begin to train a new Wotan. Already the barracks are filling with our new recruits – the cream of the Hitler Youth, young and idealistic, volunteers to a man. You and I will train them in the glorious, heroic battle tradition of our formation, for which so many brave men have died.'

He raised his voice. 'But the new Wotan will be different from the old one. It will be *our* regiment, an elite regiment run by and for us. Its only loyalty will be to Germany, the Führer and itself.' He paused to let his words take effect. 'When we return to Berlin, each and every one of you will become an NCO – *my NCOs*. All of you have fought and bled at my side. I know you all like a brother – you know me in the same way. We are comrades!'

At the exit the chocolate-coloured Rolls had still not driven away. A chain-dog had tried to move it on. But a thousand Liri note hastily thrust into his fist by the pale hand through the rear window convinced him his effort was unnecessary. Lisa stayed.

'Standard-bearer!' von Dodenburg rapped.

The young corporal carrying the Wotan black silk Death's Head banner marched forward smartly.

'Lower the standard!'

Von Dodenburg turned his burning gaze on his men again. 'Comrades, I want you – my non-commissioned officers corps – to swear this oath after me.'

He took the black silk of the banner in his left hand and raised the first two fingers of his right aloft.

'Repeat after me . . . In the name of the Führer, in the name of the Third Reich, and in the name of Wotan.'

The response came in a steady regular bass, sending the pigeons in the roof flapping wildly in alarm.

'I swear that I shall fight to the death . . . to keep our enemies from the Fatherland . . . I swear to carry out every order I am given . . . no matter what it may be.'

Von Dodenburg waited, straight and proud, for the reply to die away. 'And if I betray this oath, I shall be executed as a traitor to my Fatherland, my Führer, my comrades and the Wotan.'

'. . . my comrades and the Wotan,' a hundred harsh young voices repeated, while the watching chain-dogs stared at the haggard veterans, whom they had turfed out of Milan's red light district only a short hour ago.

Von Dodenburg nodded to the young standard-bearer. He swung round, the skull fluttering in the faint breeze.

'Captain Schwarz,' he called, 'mount up.'

Behind him the impatient hiss of escaping steam grew louder. The driver had finished his last inspection. He swung himself into the cab. Slowly the chain-dogs began to drift back to their billets. There would be no more trouble from the Wotan this night. Up in the roof, the loudspeakers burst into metallic life:

'Special train for Innsbruck, Munich, Dresden . . .'

One by one the survivors began to climb aboard.

'*Kuno!*'

Colonel von Dodenburg, watching his men embark, spun round. It was Lisa, her dark Italian eyes misted with tears, a bunch of wilting white narcissi in her hand.

'Stay,' she said brokenly.

He shook his head numbly. Behind him Schulze shouted at a big South Tyrolean farmboy who was trying to lug a looted parrot in a great gilt cage aboard.

'Come on – haul ass! And what the hell do you want that vulture for anyway? Can't you see that it's a shitting Yid – with that curved conk?'

'Screw you,' the parrot croaked.

Slowly Lisa handed von Dodenburg the drooping white flowers.

'Eh, *la guerra. Quando finira*?'

'The war – when will it be over?' he repeated slowly. 'For us of Wotan,' he said, 'it will be over when we are dead.' Gently he pressed the flowers back into her hand.

The driver sounded his whistle. It echoed mournfully through the midnight station. Slowly the special train began to draw away from the platform. Without another word, Colonel von Dodenburg turned and doubled swiftly for his compartment. A door slammed. The steam wreathed the Italian girl. She stood there, frozen like a sad grey ghost as the train gathered speed. Window after window rattled by her. A pair of red rearlights. The lights vanished in the darkness. And she was alone on the platform. The men of Wotan were on their way north to fight a new battle. It was June 6th, 1944. They would never return to Italy.